STREET SHADOWS

STREET SHADOWS

Claire Gilchrist

DUNDURN
TORONTO

Cover image: city: 123RF.com/zlajo; Coyote: shutterstock.com/Sloth Astronaut
Printer: Webcom, a division of Marquis Book Printing Inc.

Library and Archives Canada Cataloguing in Publication

Title: Street shadows / Claire Gilchrist.
Names: Gilchrist, Claire, 1983- author.
Identifiers: Canadiana (print) 20190045299 | Canadiana (ebook) 20190045787 | ISBN 9781459744714 (softcover) | ISBN 9781459744721 (PDF) | ISBN 9781459744738 (EPUB)
Classification: LCC PS8613.I41 S77 2019 | DDC jC813/.6—dc23

1   2   3   4   5   23   22   21   20   19

 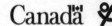 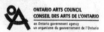

We acknowledge the support of the Canada Council for the Arts and the Ontario Arts Council for our publishing program. We also acknowledge the financial support of the Government of Ontario, through the Ontario Book Publishing Tax Credit and Ontario Creates, and the Government of Canada.

Care has been taken to trace the ownership of copyright material used in this book. The author and the publisher welcome any information enabling them to rectify any references or credits in subsequent editions.

The publisher is not responsible for websites or their content unless they are owned by the publisher.

Printed and bound in Canada.

VISIT US AT

dundurn.com | @dundurnpress | dundurnpress | dundurnpress

Dundurn
3 Church Street, Suite 500
Toronto, Ontario, Canada
M5E 1M2

ONE
LIGHT

Pica

In the beginning, all she knew was warmth and milk. Furry bodies curled around each other, squirming and straining to find the warm, sweet liquid. Everything was dark. A large, rough tongue bathed her, soothing her rising panic at being out in the world on her own. A cocoon of warm dirt protected her.

As time passed, she became more aware of where her body ended and the others began. There were three others there — others like her. When she rolled onto them, they pushed back. They wriggled around, fighting to get closer to their mother, who was not impressed. She growled at them from time to time and nipped them sharply when they bit her by accident or stepped on her tail. After a few moments of this tumbling, they would all collapse from exhaustion and lie together, listening to the sound of their breath and their mother's heartbeat.

More time passed, and she became aware of other adults besides her mother. A large female would pop her head into the den, woofing softly. Then her mother would leave for a while, and the new female would take her place, licking and soothing the pups just like a mother. She didn't have milk, but the pups kept looking and getting nipped for their efforts. They smelled a third adult too, a male, but he didn't enter the den. They could hear his soft paws circling around the entrance, and his gentle woofing greetings.

One day, her eyes opened. She looked around, blinking, seeing only light and shadow. She made out the rough outlines of her siblings, who were all fast asleep next to her mother. She slid her body out gently from underneath the heavy head of her brother and stood up, looking around. In front of her was a beautiful, bright light. Curious, she began to work her way toward it, stepping awkwardly around her siblings, who grunted sleepily as she stepped on them. Reaching the light, she realized that it was a hole leading upward, with intoxicatingly interesting smells on the other side. With determination, she pushed her chubby body upward, making her way up onto a large ledge in front of the light. She pushed her head out, and then, scrabbling with all four paws against the rocky dirt, she catapulted herself out of the hole, turning a few somersaults before coming to rest on her stomach. The light was brighter than ever, and she closed her eyes against the assault. Sounds and smells and sensations hurtled at her from all directions. It was all suddenly too much, and crying out, she tried to find her way back to the darkness. She stood up, blinking, but she couldn't see anything but the white, piercing light.

Suddenly, she smelled the adult male nearby. She heard a soft woof from above her head, and then she was picked up unceremoniously by the scruff of her neck and dumped back into the darkness. She landed on the dirt, and with a happy yelp, she burrowed her way deep into the pile of soft fur. It felt so safe and warm.

"I found a straggler," she heard from outside the hole, the male voice echoing around the walls of the den. "Trying to take her first peek out into the world."

"There is always one who just can't wait," her mother answered, tenderly licking the pup's face. "Well, my little one who wants to take the first peek. We will call you Pica."

Pica snuggled up deeper into the soft, warm fur. The adventure had exhausted her and she was content to close her eyes and relax into the safety of her mother.

Scruff

In the beginning, all he knew was warmth and milk. Furry bodies curled around each other, squirming and straining to find the warm, sweet liquid. Everything was dark. A large, rough tongue bathed him, soothing his rising panic at being out in the world on his own. A cocoon of warm dirt protected him.

As time passed, he became more aware of where his body ended and the others began. There were two others there — others like him. When he rolled onto them, they pushed back. They wriggled around, fighting to get closer to their mother, who was not impressed. She growled at them from time to time and nipped them sharply when they bit her or stepped on her tail. After a few moments of this tumbling, they would all collapse from exhaustion and lie together, listening to the sound of their breath and their mother's heartbeat.

More time passed, and he became aware of the smell of a male who was often nearby, woofing gently to his mother. The male would go away for long periods of time, and when he returned he would give a soft bark, his large head blocking the light at the entrance to the den, his smell filtering down. His mother would extricate herself gently, leaving them alone, although he could smell her nearby. In her absence, he snuggled closer to the other two pups. None of them wanted to be on the outside, and they would squirm vigorously, each trying to be in the middle of the other two. After a few moments, they would get tired and begin to mew, calling for their mother to return. And she would, taking her place beside them, curling her body around them all.

The routine was interrupted when the male stopped coming. He felt his mother becoming anxious and restless, and she began to leave them for longer and longer periods of time. When she returned, her warm milk was often difficult to get, and she became irritated as they chewed harder and harder on her nipples to try to get the milk to flow.

One day, he smelled a strange new coyote smell, and his mother jumped up, alarmed. She squeezed out of the den, and he could hear her growls mingling with the stranger's growls. All of the pups were still and frightened. After a while, it got quiet and they couldn't smell the other coyote anymore. Their mother returned to the den and snuggled around them.

As the days passed, things did not get better. His mother would leave, and it was cold. Even as he curled up next to his siblings, he no longer felt a sense of peace and safety. His stomach hurt from hunger. When his mother returned, exhausted, they would immediately begin to push against each other. What had been playful fighting in the beginning became more serious, as the pups fought desperately for what little milk there was. He found himself hurting his siblings, clawing at their faces, in order to stay close to his mother's milk source. At first, she nipped them into line, but after a few days, she stopped caring. They all grew weaker.

One day, he became aware that his mother had been gone for a very long time. The pups waited in the dark hole, listening and straining their eyes at the bright light, waiting for the darkness of her shadow to cross it. The light faded slowly and it became night, and then the light was back again. At the end of that first long day, his sister stopped moving. She had always been the smallest and weakest. Her breathing slowed, and she became cold. At the end of the second day, his brother became cold, too. Scruff lay alone in the hole, next to his two siblings, and thought about closing his eyes, too.

Instead, he stood up and started making his way toward the light at the end of the den. He walked unsteadily to the opening and slipped his body through the hole. The light was painfully bright now, and he closed his eyes against the assault. Sounds and smells and sensations hurtled at him from all directions. It was suddenly too much, and crying out, he tried to find his way back to the darkness. He stood up, blinking, but he couldn't see anything except the white, piercing light.

Moments passed and nothing happened. His breathing slowed and he found that he was able to make out shapes around him. The ground was soft under his paws, and there were large trees that cast a shadow over parts of a small clearing. Hearing a series of loud caws, he looked up to see a few dark shapes silhouetted against the light. Some birds were circling slowly above him. He stared at them, mesmerized by their steady glide. He noticed them drawing closer and closer.

He was suddenly distracted as a smell caught his attention, coming from the other side of the clearing. He began walking toward it. Although he toppled over a few times, feeling very weak, he got back up each time, standing for a few moments on shaky legs before resuming his trek. The birds continued to caw loudly, and when he glanced back up he noticed that many more of them had joined the circles.

He had just taken a few more steps when, out of nowhere, he felt something impact his back and a white-hot shot of pain ripped through his body. He fell over, crying out sharply, and looked behind him. There was nothing.

He looked around desperately, and then saw a black object hurtling toward him from the sky. Before he could react, it tore into his side, pain ripping through him again. Yelping with rage, he realized that the birds were attacking him.

His body now felt like it was on fire, and he jumped up with panic, growling and snarling in the direction of the birds. He braced himself, trying to anticipate the next attack. The crows circled patiently, a few feet from his head, waiting for the next opportunity. He shook his head as he began to feel dizzy, looking down for a moment. Then, returning his gaze to the sky, he saw a large shadow dip away from the rest, bombing straight toward him. He jumped desperately to the side, turning his head to snap and growl at it. He felt the wind of the bird's descent against his fur, but did not feel the impact this time. Looking up, he saw the bird retreating.

"Ya! Take that!" he squeaked.

He was so focused on the birds that he didn't sense the large, strange coyote standing beside him until he heard a low barking laugh. He spun around to see a tall, lanky coyote with patchy fur. Long, lean muscles stood out under his silvery coat, and his eyes carefully sized up the pup.

"A little fighter. Scrawny, but tough. I like you."

The pup stared back at him with big eyes, frozen. His back burned, his stomach contracted, and he didn't know what to do.

"I'll call you Scruff. You're a bit ragged, but you might pull through. If you survive, you can stay with me." With that, he was picked up roughly by the scruff of his neck and carried off into the dark shadows of the forest.

TWO
PLAY

Pica

"Hey, guys, check this out!" Pica called across the hillside. She grabbed the golf ball in her mouth and ran back toward her three siblings. "Ah fah a gof bah!" She found it harder to talk with the ball between her teeth. She arrived back at the den site and jumped on her brother Dane. The ball fell out of her mouth and rolled behind him. She leapt and tried to pounce on it, but missed and landed instead on his tail.

"Ouch! Quit it, Pica!" Dane growled, rolling over to his other side.

"Oops!" She shook her head, blinking a few times. The ball seemed blurry to her — that must have been why she missed it. She scratched at her eye a few times.

"What is it?" Sage asked sleepily, yawning as she cracked an eye open.

Pica forgot about her eye, seeing a potential playmate. She grabbed the ball and dropped it in front of her sister. "One of the humans left this behind — I found it down by the bushes at the bottom of the hillside," she explained. "Want to come and play with it?"

Silence. In the heat of the afternoon, all her siblings wanted to do was lie in the shade and nap.

Finally, Sage took pity on her sister. "Hey, Pica. You should nap with us now and we can play later. You know we need to rest up for our hunting lesson tonight."

"I'm not tired. I'm bored. All we ever do is lie around and nap." Pica was frustrated. She pushed the ball with her nose a few times, rolling it right in front of Dane's face. "Come on — look how cool it is!"

"Right. Cool," scoffed Kai, her other brother, from where he lay behind Dane.

Pica frowned. This was not working. "Fine. I can play a game by myself anyway." She glanced around, looking for inspiration. Her yearling sister, Taba, and her parents, Gree and Lamar, were sleeping under some bushes a few strides away. Although they were asleep, she knew that their senses were alert and they would rise at the slightest danger.

Pica took the ball in her mouth and set off up the hillside. Every few steps, she slowed and turned her head, evaluating her distance from the others. At two months old, she wasn't supposed to go very far from the den site alone, but she felt safe as long as she could see her family.

She knew that she could always yelp and they would come to help her. She crested the top of a small hill and stopped, dropping the ball onto the ground in front of her. She sat and rubbed her eye with the side of her paw. A burning feeling had started a few days ago and it didn't seem to be going away. After a good scratch, it felt a little better and she sighed with relief, looking around her.

She stood on a small dirt patch that sloped downhill. Beyond the dirt on all sides grew long, golden grasses and wildflowers. The large, open hillside was dotted with broom and heather, and sloped gently downward to a lush, green golf course, where she could see humans walking around and hitting golf balls, a sharp cracking sound punctuating the buzzing of insects. Above these noises she could hear a low, constant rumble, which her parents told her were cars and trucks on the roads nearby. All that she could see was her home, and she loved it.

Behind her was a tall wooden fence with wide slats that marked the edge of their territory. On the other side was where the humans lived. She was fascinated by them, and spent long hours in the afternoon with her face pressed up to the holes in the slats, trying to see, smell, and listen to what life was like on the other side. She was impatient to get the chance to explore beyond her home territory, but knew her parents would be furious if she went before they decided she was ready.

A bird cawed loudly, breaking her reverie, and she looked down to find the ball. It had disappeared! She ducked her head toward the dirt, sniffing around for it. She couldn't understand where it had gone. She looked around, and then spotted a patch of white in the long grass at the bottom of the slope. Surprised, she bounded down the hill and pounced on the ball. She couldn't believe how it had gotten all the way down there!

Picking it up in her mouth again, she returned to her original spot, and paying more attention this time, she dropped it in front of her. It rolled downhill — slowly at first, then picking up momentum and bouncing off the small rocks. It came to rest in the long grass at the bottom of the dirt patch.

Pica laughed, delighted. She retrieved the ball, running back up the hill with it clutched firmly in her mouth. This time, she dropped it and waited a few seconds before bounding after it, trying to trap it in her front paws before it hit the grass. She imagined herself chasing after a sleek, darting rabbit who was doing its best to evade her. She didn't have much success, but tumbling head over heels and rolling down the hill turned out to be pretty fun, too.

Although she couldn't see clearly out of one eye, she found herself improving her timing as she practised, and a few times she was able to trap the ball between her paws. She lost track of time as she played, running and pouncing.

She began to feel quite hot and tired, and decided to try one more time. She dropped the ball from the top of the hill, and waited a couple of seconds to let it pick up momentum. However, before she could set off after it, a small, scrawny, grey body hurtled past her, flying through the air after the ball. She froze when she realized that it was another young coyote, quite a bit smaller than her. His short legs peddled quickly and his thin muscles bunched up as he pounced on the ball. Trapping it cleanly between his paws, he fell sideways and slid down the rest of the hill, scrambling up and jumping to re-trap the ball as it escaped.

"Hey!" Pica was impressed. He may be small but he was clearly more agile than her.

"Hey," he said cockily, smiling and then bringing the ball back up the hill. "Want to race?"

Pica hesitated. She knew that she wasn't supposed to interact with strange coyotes. "Who are you?"

"Scruff. I just live in the forest over there." With his nose, Scruff pointed at a large forested area on the far side of the golf course. Pica sniffed him carefully and realized that she recognized his smell from the boundary between the golf course and the forest, where her family's home territory ended. She was surprised — her parents hadn't told her that there was a family with pups her age nearby.

Pica knew that other coyotes could be dangerous, but this one didn't look too scary. His thin torso was covered by a patchy, grey-brown fur coat. He had several tufts of brown fur that stuck straight up between his ears, giving him a goofy look. He held the golf ball in his mouth, his eyes asking her to play with him.

Pica smiled back. She liked the look of him. He looked fun, and she was eager to try her speed against his.

"Fine. Let's go." She watched as he dropped the ball and it began to tumble away from them.

"Ready, set, go!" she yelled as she pushed past him and raced after the ball. She felt an impact as he collided with her from the side, trying to gain positioning, and they both ended up somersaulting down the hill, missing the ball entirely. As soon as her body lost momentum, she jumped up, searching for the bright white object. She blinked a few times, her vision blurry, then noticed a spot of white behind him. She took a huge leap, clearing his body and reaching for the white with her paws. She felt only grass, and looking more closely, saw that it was just a patch of white flowers.

"You lose!" he laughed from behind her.

"Fine. Best of three!"

Pica was headed back up the hill, Scruff on her heels, when suddenly an alarm bark rang across the hillside. It was Taba, her older sister from a previous litter, and her bark was sharp and angry. Pica looked down the hill guiltily and saw her whole family at attention, tails raised, staring at her. She could just make out a low growl, probably her father, Lamar.

She turned to Scruff and poked at him with her nose. "You're not allowed here. You should probably go."

Scruff smiled at her. "All right. Thanks, it was fun, though. Maybe see you around. What was your name?"

"Pica."

"Okay, Pica. See you soon."

She watched him lope back toward the forest that marked the boundary of her family's territory. She couldn't believe that a coyote so young and scrawny would be allowed to come and go so freely. Would he be in trouble, too? Before she could think more about it, she heard her mother, a distant but angry bark.

"Pica. Get back here. Now."

Pica knew she was in trouble. Sighing, she headed back to the den, stopping to tuck the golf ball beneath a bush along the way so she could find it again. She loped back as slowly as she could, putting off the inevitable lecture. She arrived in front of her parents and dropped her tail submissively. Her ears pressed back against her head as she dropped it low.

"I'm sorry."

"You have no idea of the danger you just put yourself in." Lamar's voice was stern.

"But he was just small and —"

"Pica," Gree cut her off, "Lamar is right. You don't know anything about that other coyote. You can't talk to him, and you have to let us know if he ever crosses that line again."

"But he's not dangerous!" Pica argued, not understanding how the fun little coyote could represent a danger to her.

"He might be — how do you know? Coyotes outside our family are never our friends. That is the rule." Gree's bark was angry now. "From now on, don't go so far away on your own."

Pica sighed, turning away. Suddenly, she felt her mother give her a sharp nip on her side. She yelped in pain.

"Pica, are you taking us seriously?"

"Yes, Mom," Pica responded quickly. "I just ... he just ... seemed nice."

Her mom looked at her sternly. Then, frowning, she asked, "Pica, is your eye still bothering you?"

"A bit."

"All right. Go back to the den site and rest up. You have a big hunt tonight and you've already had a lot of excitement today. I'll be over in a minute to wash your eye again."

"Aw, Mom, it's fine," Pica said quickly, dreading her mother's rough tongue on such a sensitive area.

"It's *not* fine, Pica. You need that eye to heal or you'll never learn to hunt properly. Go now, I'll be there soon."

Pica knew she couldn't push her mother any further, and walked back to the den area, curling up under a bush to wait.

THREE
STANDOFF

Scruff

Scruff crouched, frozen, in the long grass. His front paw was raised and he listened intently, ears pointed at a spot a few steps in front of him. Above the soft breeze and bird calls, he heard a faint scratching noise and the sound of little feet crumpling the soft grass. He placed his paw carefully on the ground in front of him, barely breathing, and took another step forward. Curling his claws into the soft, loamy earth, he inhaled the faint smell of a rodent. He heard a small rustle behind him and smelled Jagger. Aware of being observed, he felt an urgent need to prove himself. Inhaling and exhaling slowly and deliberately, he pushed all the other sensory information into his periphery. He needed there to be nothing in his mind except him and the mouse. Using each nostril independently, he homed in on the position of the rodent. He heard a small squeak, which further gave away the mouse's location. Then, with a sudden tensing and releasing of his hind leg muscles, he sprung high into the air. His front legs were fully extended and his claws were splayed wide. He landed with both paws firmly on the mouse. Dropping his head, he grabbed it in his mouth and killed it triumphantly with a quick shake of his head.

He heard Jagger's gruff voice behind him. "Not bad. Killing rodents at three months is better than most pups."

Scruff turned, swelling with pride as he began to eat the mouse. He was glad that Jagger had been there to witness his successful hunt. Ever since he had been rescued from the crows, Jagger had taken care of him, supplying almost all of his food and protection. After carrying him off into the forest, he had deposited the weak little pup in a safe spot underneath a bush, and found food for him. He delicately chewed the food up and regurgitated it so the pup would be able to eat it. He watched over him for the first few days with great concern, and it wasn't until two weeks later that he began to be sure that the pup would survive.

Scruff didn't remember much of this time — it was all a blur of pain and hunger. That experience had deeply bonded him to the larger coyote, though, and he could not forget that he had a debt to repay. He still wasn't sure why Jagger had taken him in — he had been completely useless so far — but he meant to show him as soon as possible that he was able to contribute. Hopefully one day he could pay back the debt for his life.

Finishing his mouse, Scruff noticed with disappointment that Jagger had moved on. He moved around restlessly, feeling the return of a familiar sense of loneliness. He lived with a feeling of emptiness inside him most of the time, missing the family that he couldn't even remember that well. Jagger was reliable, but was a solitary male and didn't like hanging around and talking much.

Looking for something to do, Scruff set off along the edge of their forest territory, following a narrow, overgrown path that ran between the forest and the hillside, up to a large housing subdivision. There was too much daylight to forage for food near the houses, so Scruff slid behind a bush at the top of the hill and peeked out the other side, looking for the Hillside Pack.

Dane and Kai were far below, roughhousing in the shade of the hot sun. Pica was pouncing on insects, and he smiled at her intense concentration. Sage and the adult coyotes must be asleep under some bushes, because he couldn't see them. He was beginning to know this family well now — it had been two months since he first met Pica, and he watched them often. A few times, Pica had snuck away to play with him at the top of the hill, careful to return before her parents woke up. Once, she had brought her brother Dane along, and they had all played together. These were the only times that Scruff got to laugh and play, and he wanted more.

He had started to wonder if maybe the hillside adults were relenting about his presence on their territory. Even though his scent must still drift down from time to time, they hadn't issued any more alarm calls. He closed his eyes, fantasizing that he would one day be allowed to hang out with the whole family, hunting and playing with them.

His stomach growled. He was still hungry. He smelled a vole in the meadow, not far in front of him. His ears perked up, and his mouth began to water. Voles were stockier than mice, and their flesh was sweeter. He had only caught one once, because there weren't many in his forest territory. He felt his body become more alert, and his muscles twitched with excitement. He looked down the hillside again. Still no sign of the adults. The others were all absorbed in their own activities. Surely, they wouldn't notice if he crossed deeper into their territory to quickly catch a vole. He would retreat with it as soon as he had caught it.

Slowly, his body rose, and he began to stalk the rodent. He breathed in the warm air, happy to be doing something. He took a few tentative steps into the meadow and paused, waiting for the next clue. He picked up the sound of the vole again, and continued toward it gently. The other sounds and smells of the hillside dropped away and his world narrowed. All of his senses were trained on the animal. For minutes, nothing happened. He took a few steps closer. Then, he heard a warning squeak, and the vole took off down a hole.

Scruff bounded over to the hole and snuck his snout in, inhaling the musky rodent smell. He sighed. Voles were excellent diggers, and once they went back into their holes, it was virtually impossible to catch them. Suddenly, he halted. Something was wrong. He looked up, and stared straight into the eyes of the adult male from the Hillside Pack — Lamar was his name, he remembered from Pica's stories. The tall and imposing male was standing a short distance away, holding an aggressive, dominant stance, with his tail and hackles up.

Looking down at the young pup, Lamar said sternly, "You trespass. You are not allowed on our hillside."

Scruff took a few steps backwards, tail down, ready to run, and then froze. As the coyote's scent hit him, something jogged his memory. Darkness, the sounds of growls outside of his den. His mother, growling. And this growl. He tilted his head to the side, confused. But before he had time to think about it, Lamar took two steps toward him.

"This is not the first time that I have warned you to stay away. It's time —"

His voice was abruptly cut off by a thunderous growl from behind Scruff. Jagger stood at the edge of the hillside, his hackles high and his eyes glaring.

"Lamar," he snarled. "Are you threatening my pack-mate? Don't you have anything better to do than terrorize a ten-pound runt?"

"Jagger." Lamar's growl was equally threatening. "You know that this is my territory, and I'm prepared to defend it."

There was a tense pause. No one moved. Scruff felt his chest constrict, and he couldn't breathe. Jagger glanced at Scruff. "Leave. Now. I'll find you later." His voice was a command.

Scruff glanced at him, and saw the serious look in his eyes. He glanced between the two coyotes for a few more seconds, and then turned and ran back down the hill along the path, relieved to be returning to the forest. As he left, he turned his ears backwards, straining to hear, wanting to know what was happening. But all he heard were low growls, and it was impossible to make out what they were saying. He felt guilty for having started this confrontation — what if something happened to Jagger, when he was only trying to keep him safe? He arrived at the spot in the forest where Jagger usually slept and lay down in the shade, breathing hard.

Only a few minutes passed before Jagger returned, limping slightly. Scruff yelped and jumped up and touched noses with him, sniffing over the rest of his body to make sure he was otherwise unhurt.

"What happened? Are you okay? What did he say?"

Jagger gave a long sigh, lowering himself gingerly beside Scruff. "He tried to jump at me in the end, but I dodged him and ran away. I put my paw in a bit of a hole but I think it will be fine." He paused, and added bitterly, "I don't understand why he is so concerned about you — you are clearly not a threat to his precious family." He took a few long breaths, then looked down at Scruff with concern. "Scruff, you shouldn't have been there today. I haven't prepared you as I should have. You need to know that the Hillside Pack could be dangerous to you — to us. You need to stay on our side of the line."

Scruff dropped his head. "I'm sorry. I just — I like watching them play."

Jagger sighed, "It's okay. He was overreacting anyway." He hesitated, then continued. "You know, there is something that you should know about him. About them."

"What?"

"Well, it has to do with your parents."

Scruff felt his body constrict and something squeezed his heart, hard. He waited, unable to tear his eyes away from the older coyote. Suddenly, he realized that he knew what Jagger was going to say. The smell. The growl. He waited for confirmation.

"I probably should have told you earlier. I just wasn't sure how. Or when." Jagger paused, sighed, and then continued. "You've always been curious about what happened to your family, and I told you that they all died of illness. Well, with your father, that was true. He got an infection all over his body, and it eventually killed him. After that, your mother was on her own. She was already weak from giving birth. I'm sorry to have to tell you this, but Lamar and Gree — that's his mate — they took the opportunity and killed her."

Scruff sat still for a moment, stunned. "I don't understand — why?" His voice was barely a squeak.

"Territory. The golf course and hillside aren't big enough for a pack of seven. They wanted more space."

Scruff looked at him, still confused. "How do you know all this — were you there?"

"No, I wasn't. Before, I didn't have my own home territory, but this area was part of my hunting range. I knew your family pretty well, and I could see how sick your father was getting. Then, I didn't see him anymore. A few days later, I came across your mother. She was dead, and Lamar's smell was all around. It was pretty clear what had happened."

Scruff was having trouble speaking. His voice came out scratchy, and he felt like he didn't have enough air. "All this time, and I didn't know, and ..." He couldn't think of anything else to say. It hurt because it all made sense. He had smelled Lamar there, outside the den, when his mother was still alive. She must have been defending them, telling him to go away. He must have waited for the right opportunity, and then — he couldn't continue the thought.

Scruff jumped up and paced away from Jagger. He felt suddenly furious. Whirling back at him, he glared at him. "Why are you telling me this now? Why didn't you tell me before?" He thought back to the number of hours he had watched over the Hillside Pack, wishing he was part of their close-knit family. The whole time he had been ignorant that they were responsible for the death of his own family.

Jagger looked at him gently. "Scruff, I'm sorry. You're so little, I didn't want you to be so upset and angry. I didn't want you to do something dumb like try to get revenge on them before you were ready. You've always been quite stubborn and I wanted to make sure you were old enough when you learned the truth."

"I'll kill them."

"I knew you would want to. But you are still too young. Get stronger, have patience, and one day I'll help you get your revenge."

Scruff sighed and walked over to him, licking his chin. "Thanks, Jagger."

Jagger looked at Scruff with a long, calculating look, replying, "Remember, I'm here to help."

FOUR
THREAT

Pica

Worried, Pica watched her father and mother return back down the hill from the shade of the bushes where Taba had made her and her siblings hide. She hadn't been able to see much of what was going on, but Taba and Gree were both very worried, and just a moment ago, Gree had gone to see if Lamar needed help. She had only been gone a minute when they both returned. As he approached, Taba gave the all-clear bark and all of the pups catapulted themselves into the open. They surrounded Lamar, pelting him with questions.

"Who was that?"

"What did he want?"

"Why was he in our territory?"

"What happened?"

"Quiet." Lamar stopped them with a short bark. He glanced at Gree, pausing before continuing.

"We probably should have talked to you about this before, but we weren't sure that it was going to become a problem." He paused again, exchanging another glance with Gree. Pica wondered what they were saying to one another with their wordless looks. Finally, Lamar began to explain. "The coyote who trespassed onto our home territory is named Jagger. Before he adopted Scruff, he was a solitary male whose hunting territory overlapped with ours. Of course, he stayed clear of our home territory, but when we were hunting in our larger territory, we crossed paths with him a few times. He mainly avoided us.

"Things have been changing quickly this year. The biggest difference is that he started defending the forest area as his home territory. Usually, solitary coyotes don't defend a home territory, but he has formed a sort of pack with that little pup, and now they are around a lot more often."

"Who did the forest belong to before Jagger?" Kai spoke up, confused.

"The Forest Pack lived there for as long as we have been here. We never had any problems with them. But when they died, Jagger took control. We weren't sure how it would go because we didn't know him very well. But ever since he has taken over the forest, he has been getting more and more aggressive. Today you saw that he trespassed onto our territory and challenged us directly."

"He backed down, though, right?" Taba questioned, worry in her voice.

"Of course," Lamar asserted. "I'm bigger and stronger than he is. He doesn't want to risk getting injured. But I don't trust him."

Pica cocked her head to the side. It didn't quite make sense to her. "But what happened to the Forest Pack? And where did Scruff come from?"

Gree exchanged glances with Lamar, and then looked at her pups. "The most important thing to know is that Jagger and Scruff could both be very dangerous, and you all need to stay very close to us."

Pica was not satisfied with that answer. "But what happened to them?"

Gree looked at her sharply. "You don't need to know any more. Jagger is very dangerous, and he poses a direct threat to our family. You need to follow our directions and stay close to us."

Pica sighed, feeling her heart sink. "What do you mean by 'stay close'?"

"Stay close means *stay close*. No more wandering, meeting strange coyotes and playing with them. Stay here with your siblings and practise your hunting. You, especially, need to practise. Hunting hasn't been going well for you so far."

Her tone was stern, and Pica didn't want to pick a fight. Her mother worried about her almost constantly. A few months ago, just after she met Scruff, her eye had gone from itchy, to burning, to swollen shut over the course of just a few days. Then there was a difficult period of time that she couldn't remember well. Finally, after many days, the pain went away, and she woke up able to open her eye again. However, the world no longer looked the same. She stumbled over her feet, ran into things, and pounced to the side of prey she was trying to trap. Her head hurt all the time.

Now, almost two months later, she had started to do better. She had regained her coordination and she experienced fewer headaches. However, she was the only one of all her siblings who had yet to successfully catch a prey animal. She felt guilty knowing that her parents worried about her so much when they had other things to take care of. Sighing, she wandered over to a nearby bush and lay down for a nap.

Later that day, Pica was feeling bored, and decided to go for a walk toward the golf course where her parents were relaxing in a shady spot, out of view of the golfers. She figured that as long as she was between Taba and her parents, she could explore a little bit without breaking the new rules. She wandered aimlessly, enjoying the feeling of the sun on her fur and watching the humans swing their sticks and hit the little white balls across the grass. She was careful to stay hidden, and stopped at a few small, scrubby trees to eat the caterpillars that climbed up their trunks. She couldn't stop thinking about what her parents had said earlier. What had happened to the Forest Pack? Where did Scruff come from? She was deep in thought when her ears picked up her mother's voice. She couldn't make out the words, so she crept a little bit closer, tucking in behind a small bush.

Gree's voice was low and urgent. "Of course we are going to stay away from the forest territory. But I think the problem is leaving one adult behind with the pups. They're still so small."

Pica froze, listening intently. The low bush separated her from her parents, and because the wind was blowing strongly into her face, they weren't going to smell her. She kept listening.

"I know," Lamar responded quietly. "But we can't feed everyone for long if we stay on the hillside. We will need to teach them to cross the road."

"I know." Gree sighed. "I just think it is too soon. The road is so dangerous — I don't think they're ready yet."

"I don't know how much longer we can wait."

There was a long silence. Finally, Gree spoke. "We could take care of Jagger before anything else happens."

"You know that a confrontation with him could seriously injure one of us. He has killed before. I think it's too dangerous."

"I know." Gree sounded tired. "It's just that I have a bad feeling about this. I don't trust him."

"We'll figure out something."

Pica heard her mother sigh heavily again. Then, she heard her parents stand to stretch, and was suddenly worried that they would discover her on their return to the den site. She began to back away, retracing her steps as quickly as possible until she got closer to her siblings.

Then she lay down, pretending to be sleepy and relaxed. But beneath her calm exterior, her body hummed with thoughts and questions. Who had Jagger killed? Why would her parents not tell the pups about the Forest Pack? She vowed to try to find out more.

Over the next month, there was no sign of Jagger, and the pups had to stay so close to the adults that Pica couldn't sneak away to try to find Scruff. Each night, two adults stayed behind with the pups while only one went on patrol. This didn't work very well, because food was more difficult to find on the golf course than it was in their larger hunting territory. As the days passed, Jagger seemed like less and less of a threat, and they all thought more and more about their hunger. Finally, one night, it came to a head.

The sun had dipped below the hill and the cool air had set in. The golf course had shut down and the pups were preparing to go hunting on the green with Taba and Gree. Lamar was about to leave on patrol.

"Hey, Mom," Kai began. "How come you still have to watch over us like that? Jagger isn't around, and it isn't like we are tiny puppies anymore."

Taba broke in with a snort. "You are not even close to full-grown yet, and there is no way you would stand a chance against a large male like Jagger."

Pica couldn't help herself, and chimed in. "Well, even if we still have to stay together, maybe it's time for us to try leaving the hillside — we could try hunting in the streets." She held her breath, wondering if she had gone too far.

Gree looked at her with a sigh and a smile. "I'm not surprised that you suggested that — I think you've been ready to cross streets since you were born. But yes, in fact, we have been talking about it and it is probably time."

"All right!" Kai jumped up, throwing himself at Dane in excitement. "Streets! Houses! Finally!"

Sage joined in, and then all of the puppies were jumping and growling at each other joyfully. They could barely contain their excitement. Before they could get started, however, they had to wait for the deepest, darkest part of the night, when the fewest cars would be on the roads. They waited impatiently, listening to their mother drone on with specific road descriptions and instructions.

"It is the most dangerous thing you'll ever do. More dangerous than other coyotes. More dangerous than humans." She spoke gravely. "You need to be brave, and *never, ever* let yourself freeze in fear."

"It's pretty dark — can we go now?" Kai was always very excited when it came to a new and dangerous adventure.

"Just about. We should wait just a few more minutes," Gree said. "Then it will be easier for us to become shadows. But before we go, there is just one last thing we need to talk about."

The pups jumped up and began to crowd Gree and Lamar, knowing that they were minutes away from leaving. Pica jumped in closer, accidentally stepping on Kai's tail.

"Hey — watch where you're stepping," he snapped.

"Watch your tail then," Pica snapped back, impatient to get going.

"Why do you always —"

"Hey." Lamar's growl interrupted them. "That's exactly what we need to talk about. You all need to control your excitement. If you act heedlessly, you could get killed. Pica, Kai, you two, especially. No messing around by the side of the road."

"Sorry," they both mumbled. Pica felt anxious — could she remember to follow all the instructions?

"Okay," Lamar continued, "beyond the rules we have talked about, it is important that you grasp the concept of not just moving through the night, but *being* the night. When you leave our safe haven, it is important that you learn to blend into the night. We don't want to be detected by any humans out there. Humans are unpredictable and dangerous. You shouldn't move when they pass by, whether it is in a car, on a bike, or on foot. You must press your body against something and be completely still — you have to become part of its shadow. When you are outside this place, you must not be a living, breathing body. You are a street shadow."

The pups listened, intently. Then Kai ran over to a bush.

"Check it out! I'm a shadow!" Then he froze.

He was joking, but Pica tried closing her eyes and then opening them again, and found that he had all but disappeared. The soft blending of his fur from brown to silver and the furry edge of his profile helped him to disappear completely into the grey palette of the bush behind him. She smiled as she understood what her father had been talking about.

"All right, very nice, Kai. Okay, I think we're ready. Now, one last time — what are the three rules you have to follow no matter what?"

Sage piped up quickly. "One — no humans. We don't exist for them. Two — don't mess around when we are crossing the roads. The machines are very fast and we have to learn to cross at the right time. Three — don't talk to other coyotes until we are bigger. And don't pick fights with anything too big."

Gree nodded her head. "Good. Everyone got it? Most important, you must promise to obey us, whatever we say. No matter what it is."

Pica thought that sounded a little extreme, but all of her siblings were nodding their assent, so she nodded, too.

Gree's eyes picked her out and stared at her, laser sharp. "Pica? No matter what?"

"Yes, Mom."

"Okay, let's go. I'll go first. Lamar will take the back. Stay together. Taba — you want to come, too?"

"I can't handle the watching," Taba replied, stress lacing her voice. "I'll do my own thing and meet you all back here later." She gave them all one last glance. "Good luck!" she called out as she turned and loped away. Everyone else headed out toward the road.

FIVE
CROSSING

Pica

Pica repeated the three rules to herself as she followed her family. No humans. No fooling around. No other coyotes. It all seemed so simple, but she still had so many questions. What made humans so dangerous? How fast did you need to move across the road to avoid the cars? What were the other coyotes like — and could she really not talk to any of them? She hoped that she would find out the answers to all her questions soon.

They reached the rock wall that served as the border between the hillside and the road. As Pica scrambled over it, she realized how much bigger she was than the last time she had stood next to it. Now she was able to jump nimbly to the top and scramble down the other side. She joined her family, who was huddled under some bushes by the side of the road. Pica squirmed to the front beside her mother, and peered into the darkness.

"You never just cross," Gree instructed. "Find a place to wait, and listen carefully. Feel that? That rumble in the ground that you can feel in your paws means a car is coming. Now you can hear it. Here it comes —"

Pica looked down the road and saw a blinding spot rushing straight at her. It almost seemed like it would mow the bushes over, with their whole family in its path. She fought the urge to close her eyes, staring hard as the car whipped past them with a few feet to spare. She heard Sage yelp in fear. The branches on the bushes whistled back and forth as the wake hit them.

"There, it's over. So you have to learn to not be afraid of that. The cars stay on the pavement. You need to stay off the pavement until you are sure it is safe. We'll go in two groups." Gree looked back, thinking. Another car whipped by, and this time it didn't scare Pica as much. She looked at it as it passed, exchanging smiles with Kai. "Okay, dare-devils," Gree continued, nodding at Pica and Kai with a smile. "You come first. Dane and Sage, go next with Lamar."

Pica's heart jumped. She grinned at Kai, who grinned back nervously. At that moment a truck roared past, louder and brighter than the previous two cars. Both Pica and Dane jumped. "Look and listen. Feel the vibrations with your paws. All clear?" Gree asked them.

Pica waited. All she felt was her own breath, coming sharply in and out of her lungs. "All clear," she replied.

"Okay, one … two … three … NOW." Gree barked with an intensity that they could not ignore. All three coyotes scrambled up to the pavement and galloped across the road. Pica couldn't look to the side, not wanting to see a bright light bearing down on her. She didn't even breathe in, begging her muscles to work harder and harder. Just as she reached the other side, she tripped over something on the road and somersaulted forward. Regaining her balance quickly, she dove off the side of the road, rolling into the bushes. Kai rolled down after her and landed on her. They laughed in relief.

"Wow. That was scarier than I thought it would be," Pica told him.

"Ha — that was nothing!" Kai replied with a grin.

"That is not true! You were totally scared!" Pica jumped on him as she said this.

"Pica!" Gree growled at her. "Don't mess around. And with your bad eye, you need to concentrate harder. You can't be tripping over your feet when you're on the road. Next time, I want you to breathe more deeply and try to be a bit calmer."

Pica scrambled to a sitting position, suddenly serious, looking intently across the road. She knew her mother was right — she needed to be twice as good as her siblings to make up for her eye. The others waited on the far side for the right moment. Pica watched and listened. "Don't do it. Not yet," she whispered. The rumbling feeling intensified and a truck passed with a howl. She held her breath, hearing Lamar give the all-clear to the other two. The second group scrambled across the road safely,

Kai and Sage having a similar reaction to their siblings, laughing with relief.

"The first time is always the worst," said Gree. "Now, let's go exploring. Stay close!"

They set out along a footpath and hit a road that was rimmed on either side by a deep ditch. "We stay in the ditch — it's dry this time of year," called Lamar as he jumped down. They loped along in the ditch, occasionally having to pop up onto the street to cross a road. The roads were very quiet, and only a few times did Lamar bark, "Down! Freeze!" And they would all crouch in the ditch as the car passed, its headlights illuminating the road. Once, they came across a crowd of humans, who were walking and talking loudly. Following Gree and Lamar's lead, the pups crouched in the ditch, not moving, and the humans walked right past them, just a few feet away. As they faded into the distance, Pica let out her breath. She couldn't believe that they hadn't been detected. The humans seemed so clumsy and stupid for creatures who were so powerful.

Lamar led them along in the ditch until they got to a wide expanse of pavement leading up to a series of large, low metal buildings. He stopped to face them. "As you travel, you have to be very careful where you go. We'll teach you where it is safe to go — this city has many other coyotes, and they will defend their territory. At first, make sure you stick to the places we show you — no coyotes are defending them. As you get bigger, you can decide for yourself where you want to go. And always keep your eyes peeled for dangers — other coyotes, humans, dogs, anything that moves, really." He paused, making sure they were listening.

"This area is sometimes a good place to find rats. Spread out, and try hunting on your own. Remember what I have always told you. You have to put yourself into the mind of the animal you are trying to catch. What is their mood? What are they doing? You must anticipate their moves and be one step ahead of them."

Pica set off to hunt, but an hour passed with no luck. A few times she got close, but either made some kind of a small noise that alerted the rat to her presence or missed it on the pounce. When she heard Gree's bark to come back together again, she trotted back, frustrated. She was the last one to arrive, and she could hear her siblings talking excitedly about their kills. As they found increasing success hunting, she felt more and more sensitive about her failure. Would her eye injury stop her from ever learning how to hunt? And if that happened, would her family continue to take care of her when she was an adult? She didn't think they would be able to, especially next spring when there were new mouths to feed.

"How did it go, Pica?" Sage looked at her with a hopeful smile.

Pica hesitated. "Great! I caught one!" Even as she said it, she felt ashamed. As her siblings pelted her with questions, she had to quickly make up her story. At the end, she saw Gree looking at her carefully, head cocked, but her mother said nothing.

Pica quickly suggested, "Let's keep going." She was relieved when her parents nodded and took the lead again.

Over the next few hours, the family made a wide arc, slowly returning to their starting point. Pica's head swam with all the new things she had seen. She learned how to hide under a parked car when a human walked past if there was no ditch. Taba showed them how to find edible food in the humans' backyard gardens. Kai found a dead raccoon, and they all learned that if something smells really bad, it could be dangerous to eat it. It was still dark when they reached the first road again, but all of the pups were ready to go home. They were exhausted.

This time, Gree made them cross one at a time, each checking with her when they thought it was safe and then scrambling across. Pica went first again, more confident this time. At the other edge of the road, instead of diving into the bushes, she jumped gracefully off the embankment and turned around to watch her siblings. Dane was next, followed by Kai, and she was proud at how confident and strong they both looked. She felt older somehow, as if crossing the road had also caused them to cross an invisible line between puppyhood and independence.

As Sage prepared to cross, Pica frowned. She could see her sister's face, and it showed only terror. She crouched for about a minute by the roadside, seemingly frozen. Nothing passed. Finally, she said hesitantly, "Now?"

"Go now," replied Lamar.

"Okay …" she responded weakly. She took a step, then paused.

"NOW!" commanded Gree. Pica could feel a gentle rumble. It was still around the corner, but Sage had to start moving immediately.

"Okay ..." she repeated, taking a few more steps into the road. The truck's lights flashed around the corner, and all of a sudden time seemed to speed up. Sage was illuminated in the headlights as the truck hurtled toward her.

"GO, Sage! Now!" Pica cried as the truck bore down on her sister. Sage looked at her and something seemed to unlock. She scrambled awkwardly across the rest of the road and dove into the ditch as the truck roared past. Gree and Lamar followed immediately after.

"What happened there, Sage?" Gree questioned sharply.

"I don't know. I just ... couldn't move." Sage walked over to Pica and nuzzled her.

"Don't let it happen again." Gree paused, breathing hard. "Okay, I bet you are all tired — let's go home."

As Pica followed her mother back, she breathed in the cool, fresh air and felt the sounds and smells of the city fade away. She hadn't realized before just how lucky they were to live in this oasis — it was calm and peaceful, and they were able to see danger from far away. She wondered, after having travelled through the city for the first time, what it was like for all the other coyotes who lived in abandoned lots and under small bushes in big backyards. She couldn't imagine them having the chance to lie around in the sun and play with golf balls.

With thoughts of cars, dogs, and raccoons, the pups snuggled deep under the bushes and fell fast asleep.

SIX

CONSTRUCTION

Scruff

A deep rumbling in the earth woke Scruff late one morning as he napped in the sun. He had been in the middle of a wonderful dream, where the forest floor was carpeted with fat squirrels, each one slower and fatter than the last. As he raced toward them, gaining ground, the forest floor began to rumble, shaking him off his feet. His eyes opened and a second later, he realized that the ground was actually moving.

He jumped to his feet, alert. He could feel the rumbling in the ground through the pads of his paws and up into his legs. It seemed like something very large was approaching — something dangerous. He dove deeper into the bushes for cover, his heart beating quickly. The noise was loud, but after a few moments, he realized that it wasn't getting any closer. He listened for a few more minutes, and, as his pulse slowed, he began to approach the noise.

As he got closer, he was able to distinguish different sounds. There was a screech of metal, a high whirring noise, and a rhythmic low thump. When he arrived at the edge of the forest, he gasped. The normally quiet road that bordered the forest on the opposite side of the hillside and golf course was crawling with trucks and machines! He had never seen anything like it before. They looked like terrifying, large predators with high, craning metal necks and steel jaws. The wheels at the base were as high as a small tree. Humans roamed everywhere, talking to each other and walking around the machines.

Scruff stayed there for hours, trying to make sense of it all. The activity level and noise would rise and fall, but the machines showed no sign of leaving. Then, Jagger was beside him, crouching low and watching. Scruff noticed that Jagger's ears were pressed back flat against his head in fear and anxiety, and realized that his ears were doing the same thing. He was glad to see him.

"Jagger — what's going on?"

Jagger looked over at him grimly. "It's a construction site. They are going to build something. Probably houses."

"On the road?"

"No. They're going to build here, where we live."

Scruff looked around, his eyes wide. "But this is our forest!"

"It won't be our forest for long. They'll cut down the trees to make room for the houses."

"How do you know?"

"I've seen it before."

They were silent, each lost in thought. Scruff didn't want to voice the question, but eventually whispered, "So what are we going to do?"

"I don't know."

Scruff had never heard Jagger sound so sad before. Jagger had never talked about his life before adopting Scruff, always brushing off questions, saying he didn't want to think about it. Scruff wondered if something like this had happened to him before. He turned his head to ask, but saw Jagger's defeated expression and decided against it.

From that moment on, Jagger declared the forest to be unsafe, and began sleeping under the porch of an abandoned house in the housing development. Scruff didn't immediately follow him. He didn't understand why they had to leave so soon — the forest was still fine.

However, over the next month, the machines began to systematically destroy the forest. First, whirring blades felled many of the trees, leaving just a thin strip between the construction site and the hillside. Next, big machines came in and removed the dirt and rocks, clawing a huge, gaping hole in the earth. One day, Scruff watched in horror as they clawed up his family's old den site. He lay under the cover of a nearby bush and watched as a machine drove right over his den, clearing out all of the bushes and trees. When they had finished, he could barely recognize it. After the humans had gone home, he crept into the area, desperately searching for the hole where he had been born. The new, more powerful smells of the humans and machines had completely obliterated any scents that may have remained, and he was unable to find the familiar landmarks. He sat down and turned his face to the sky, howling his anger and sadness. This was the last connection he'd had to his family, and it was now gone forever.

The next day, the humans put up a large fence all the way around the site, leaving the strip of trees between the hillside and the construction site, but walling off the rest of the area. Scruff realized sadly that Jagger had been right — the forest was truly destroyed. He watched all day as the humans worked industriously, his heart aching. When night fell, he found himself unable to leave the area. He located a small gap in the fencing, biting and tearing at it to create a slightly larger hole, big enough for him to squeeze through. That night, he prowled through the entire construction area, trying to locate any of the places he had once known. Everything was unrecognizable.

As dawn began to light the area and the sun threatened to rise, he left the fenced construction site and padded slowly in the direction of the housing subdivision, feeling completely defeated. Following Jagger's instructions, he located the house and slipped into the backyard. Tall weeds grew up to his shoulders, and the human smells were so stale that he almost couldn't detect them. Jagger was curled up in a ball under the sagging back porch, and although he must have been aware of Scruff's arrival, he did not raise his head. Crouching down, Scruff entered the damp darkness, turning a few times before curling up into a miserable ball, tucking his nose underneath his tail.

Every few minutes, a new noise startled Scruff. There were loud whirring sounds, car doors slamming, and frequent dog barking. It was much less quiet and peaceful than the forest, and it smelled damp and mouldy under the deck. It was slightly wet under his stomach, making him feel cold. He repositioned himself a few times, still feeling unsettled.

"Jagger?"

"What," was the muffled reply.

"I don't like this spot. I can't sleep — it's so loud."

Jagger raised his head, irritated. "Then leave — go find yourself a better spot, see if I care," he snapped.

Scruff was hurt by the sharp words, and crawled out from under the porch immediately, shaking out his fur. There had to be a better place somewhere. He squinted. The sun was fully up now and the streets were full of light. He almost turned back to the porch, but didn't want to seem weak, so he confidently headed out of the yard and down the back alley. He would go and find a better spot, and Jagger would be thankful.

He wandered down the alley, trying to stay close to the fences and trash cans, hiding whenever he heard a car coming. He wasn't used to being out on the streets in the daylight. He stopped to sniff each house he passed, but they all showed signs of recent human activity. The narrow alley opened onto a larger street, and he stepped out, suddenly feeling very exposed. He heard barking and saw a small dog pulling at the end of a leash about a half block away. He grinned, knowing the dog was not much of a threat, but then jumped back as the woman on the end of the leash picked up the dog and started screaming at him. He took off down the street away from them, but then skidded to a halt as a car backed out of a driveway in front of him. The honk of the horn was deafening. He felt like he was being attacked on all sides by strange and unexpected things. He realized that coming out here was a terrible mistake, and fled back into the safety of the alley.

Scruff was too stubborn to return to the abandoned house so quickly, so he decided to head back to the construction site. He found a clump of trees at the edge of the golf course and fell into a fitful sleep, woken every few minutes by a loud thump or screech from the machines.

Night finally fell again, and Scruff returned to the abandoned house, exhausted. When he arrived, he saw that Jagger had already taken off on his nightly patrol. Sighing, Scruff did a quick tour of the trash cans and then returned to the porch, curling up in the darkness. He was still hungry, but was too tired to explore anymore. When Jagger returned later that night, he didn't seem at all surprised to see the pup there. He crawled over next to Scruff and licked the side of his face.

"It doesn't seem so bad here anymore, does it?" he asked, grinning.

"It's tough," Scruff replied. "Is there anywhere else we can go?"

"Not really. This isn't the first time I've been forced to leave my home ..." Jagger paused here, his grin fading before continuing. "Anyway, before I adopted you, I lived alone for a few years. I didn't have a home territory, because I didn't really need one on my own, you know? No one to meet up with at the end of the day." His face was sad. He looked away for a moment, coughing, and then his voice returned to its normal gruffness.

"I've been a lot of places. Just about everywhere that is livable has a coyote or a pack that has staked out their home territory already. It didn't used to be that way, but now it seems like there are more and more coyotes around. It isn't easy to find new territory. You have to live somewhere terrible or get really lucky. All across the city, nowhere is as peaceful and nice as this area. Around here, it's quiet, and the humans don't bother you. Lots of food. You have no idea how good we have it here."

"So, what are we going to do?"

"Well, I guess we can stay at this house for a while, but more humans will probably move in eventually.... There is another option." He glanced at Scruff, his eyes narrowed. "We could fight for a new spot. Of course, with the risk of getting hurt, it would have to be really nice to make it worth it."

Scruff's eyes widened. He had a good idea what Jagger was referring to.

"You know," Jagger's voice darkened, "they are responsible for the death of your family."

Scruff found himself breathing more quickly, anger mixed with fear. "But there are seven of them and —"

"No one said we have to fight them all at the same time." Jagger's eyes glowed in the darkness, and he seemed excited.

Scruff stared at him, and then shook his head. "I don't know, maybe we should look around the city a bit — you know, you probably missed something. I'm sure there is somewhere we could live."

Jagger scoffed, "Sure, Scruff. I'm sure we'll find another quiet forest just down the road." He shook his head. "No. It's time you grow up. Either you stand up for what you deserve and take on the coyotes who killed your mother, or it's time for us to go our separate ways."

Scruff looked at him pleadingly. "Jagger, I don't want to leave you."

"Well, then help me get us a new home territory. Listen, just think about it, okay? I'm not saying that we have to kill them. But there are other ... options," he said, his voice trailing off mysteriously.

"Okay," Scruff replied quietly. His mind raced as he wondered how he would ever survive if Jagger left him on his own. Jagger turned away from him then, curling up into the dirt and beginning to nap. Scruff lay down, too, feeling cold and alone, unable to sleep.

SEVEN

DONUT

Pica

For a few weeks, Pica continued to cross the busy road and explore the city with her family. Although it was going well, she could feel her anxiety rising with each day. She still hadn't been able to catch her own prey, and she could see that her parents were getting more and more worried, though they tried not to show it. She had lied a few times about catching something when no one was looking, but she wasn't sure that anyone believed her anymore.

Things became worse when large machines invaded the nearby forest. The rumblings and musty human smells hung in the air. Now, all that remained as a buffer between their territory and the construction site was a thin strip of trees.

Pica couldn't stop thinking about this disturbance and worrying about Scruff. She hadn't smelled him on any of her family's hunting missions, and wondered if something had happened to him. She wanted to look around more at night, when the machines were quiet, but Gree and Lamar had forbidden the pups to go there, and avoided the area themselves.

Pica's siblings seemed to accept this situation, trusting their parents to protect them. However, Pica was unsatisfied. If the machines had dug up most of the forest already, how did her parents know that they had finished their destructive march? What would stop them from pushing through the last few trees and into their home?

One day dawned especially hot for autumn. That afternoon, as the sun beat down on the meadow, her fur itched and she felt restless. Even ducking under a large bush and digging down into the dirt didn't completely cool her off. Looking around, she saw her family asleep, spread out under various bushes around the meadow. Now that they were more than half of their adult size, and the threat of Jagger had passed, the pups were not required to always stay so close to the adults.

Pica turned over and tried to nap for about an hour or so. Hearing an especially loud screech of metal, she opened her eyes and raised her head. Feeling an itch in her back leg, she rolled out from under the bush for a good stretch and scratch, and then stood for a few moments, looking around. Her family continued to nap, undisturbed by the noises. She began to walk slowly, skirting the side of the forest, staying on their side of the neutral path. Using each nostril independently, she focused on the construction site, separating out the individual smells that wafted her direction, analyzing them with curiosity. She picked out sweat, humans, machines, oil, and the musty smell of the deep earth.

Suddenly, sliding in underneath the usual smells, she sensed something that she had never smelled before. It reminded her of human food she had found once on the golf course, but it had a sweetness that she had never before sensed. The smell was very faint and with the next gentle breeze she lost it. It was definitely coming from the direction of the construction site. She took a few more steps, coming to the edge of the golf course and straining to smell what was happening through the trees. She picked up the sweet scent again, and noticed her mouth beginning to water.

Taking one more look around, Pica decided to take a very quick peek. She entered the small patch of trees, threading her way between two large hemlocks. The air was immediately cooler, and the ground was soft under her feet. She sniffed carefully for any signs of Jagger. There was nothing. She did pick up the scent of an unknown coyote, but it was old. She saw a narrow path in front of her and followed it, winding around a few thick bushes. The cooler forest air invigorated her, and she suddenly felt very awake. Moments later, she arrived at the edge of the construction site. In front of her was a thick wire fence, and she saw that there was a small opening between two sections of the fence. Trying to get a better view of the machines, she carefully squeezed through the opening and jumped under a large bush on the other side. Squirming forward on her belly, she peered out between the branches and leaves.

Narrowing her eyes against the bright sun, she saw a small, low building in front of her. She waited a few moments, listening attentively, and then trotted closer to it, peering around the side. She gasped at the sudden on-slaught of shapes and colours. It was chaos, and it was difficult for her to know what she was looking at. She flattened her ears against her head to try to muffle the screeching. She focused on the machine closest to her. It was a large, metallic beast, bigger than some of the build-ings in the golf course, and it was scooping dirt and rocks from a large pile, dropping them into a hole. Farther away, several machines with enormous wheels drove back and forth, emitting a series of shrieking beeps. Most surpris-ing was a mammoth structure rising out of the hole in the earth. Rows and rows of metal bars created the skeleton of a large cube several times larger than the largest build-ing Pica had ever seen. Her parents hadn't said anything about a skeleton — she would have to tell them about this.

She was about to turn around to quickly return to the safety of the hillside when suddenly that unique, sweet smell drifted back into her consciousness. Flaring her nostrils, she zeroed in on the source. A short distance from her, on the side of the building, was a small set of stairs leading to a door. There, sitting on the bottom step, was a large, sweet-smelling box. She knew she shouldn't

go any farther, but she suddenly had the urge to bring some back for her family. They were always the ones to provide for her — wouldn't it be great if she could come back and share something new and delicious with them?

Pica checked again for human movement or sound. She stayed still for a moment, all senses alert. She knew that it would be better to leave now, while she was safe. However, she didn't sense any humans nearby, and the smell coming from that box was so tempting. With a final look around, she followed the edge of the building until she reached the stairs.

The smell was much stronger now and she was able to pick out new elements — ripe fruit, and something she couldn't quite identify. She bumped the box gently with her nose. It fell over on its side, causing her to jump back with surprise. A few objects tumbled out of it onto the ground, and Pica lowered her head to inspect them. They were round and lightly coloured, and as she breathed in a fine powder blew into her nostrils, causing her to sneeze. She took a tentative bite. It gave way easily in her jaws, dissolving into her mouth with a sweet, sticky sensation. She closed her eyes in bliss. Swallowing, she lowered her head and took a bigger bite, noticing a sticky fruit sub-stance exploding out of the object as she ate it.

Smells and sounds faded away. Each bite revealed a new sensory adventure. She was so focused on the smells and tastes that she didn't immediately register the crunch-ing of heavy feet on gravel. Suddenly, there was a loud shout. Pica whipped her head up and saw human feet in front of her. Standing at the corner of the building were

three large men. Panic stopped her breath and she froze, staring at them. The only thing her brain registered was the fact that these men were standing directly between her and the fence.

One of the men shouted again, taking a step toward her. His movement unlocked something in Pica and she found herself able to flee. She dodged to the side and tried to turn back toward the gap in the fence, but the men were just a few feet away from it and she veered away in fear. Wheeling around, she ran along the line of the fence, away from the men, desperately looking for another exit. She took a few more strides, searching the fenceline in desperation, when suddenly she became aware of something blocking her path. She skidded to a stop as her face hit another fence. She had reached a corner and was blocked in on two sides. She whirled, feeling trapped.

"Help!" Her voice was a puppy yelp. She leapt up the fence, trying to climb it, her paws scrabbling to find something to cling to, but she fell back down into the dirt. Her head whirled as she saw machines and men approaching her from all sides.

"Over here!" The bark was familiar. Pica looked toward the sound and saw Scruff staring at her from the other side of the fence. He was bigger and skinnier than when she had seen him last, but the tufts of fur sticking up from between his ears were unmistakable, as was his smell. He pointed with his nose to a small hole in the fence that she had missed the first time she raced past it. She bounded to the spot and flung her body underneath.

The hole was lopsided and one of the metal prongs snagged her side. She yelped with pain and tried to move forward, but she was stuck. She could hear a machine growling louder and louder, and felt the dust hitting her fur. She didn't have long now — it sounded like it was almost on top of her.

With a long, high howl, she dug her back claws into the soft earth and pushed hard. The metal piece scraped down her side, ripping into her skin, but she slid through to the other side. She jumped up and leapt into the safety of a bush. The noise of metal wrenching against itself sounded loudly behind her and she exited the far side of the bush, running blindly. She finally stopped in the shadow of a tall hemlock, breathing hard, and looked back to make sure that the humans weren't pursuing her. She only saw Scruff, trotting after her.

"Scruff!" she said, panting. She craned her neck backwards to investigate the cut on her side, and felt that it was wet with blood. She looked up again and her eyes met the angry eyes of Scruff.

"Why are you here?" he asked, his voice accusatory.

"I was worried about the construction, and worried about you. Are you mad at me?"

He huffed angrily. "This is *my* forest."

Pica tilted her head to look at him. "Scruff, what's wrong?" She couldn't understand what had changed since they had last played. His eyes didn't look the same. They looked cold.

Scruff looked down. "I don't want to talk about it. I don't want to ever see you again."

Pica frowned. "I don't understand. But I need to ask you something important. It's about Jagger."

Scruff raised his eyes to her suspiciously. "What?"

"I haven't seen you since — well, I overheard my parents talking about him. They said he has killed before. I was worried about you —"

"Don't be." Scruff's face hardened. "I don't believe anything your parents say. Jagger was the one who rescued me, not them. And —"

Just then, a familiar scent blew through the air and they both froze.

Scruff looked at her and shook his head. "He's coming. You should get out of here, quickly," he whispered urgently.

The danger was imminent. She had no time to lose. If he were to catch her here ... she shuddered. Without waiting another second, she whirled and took off back toward home, her side hurting sharply as she lengthened her stride.

She ran blindly without looking where she was going. Branches whipped her face and her paws stumbled on rocks. *Run ... run ... run*, coursed through her mind. She missed a root sticking out and tripped, rolling a few times before jumping back up and dizzily continuing her flight. A few moments later she sensed light, and then she broke out into the corner of the hillside. She risked a glance behind her. Nothing moved. She slowed to a lope, breathing hard and tucking back into the bushes that surrounded the golf course. As her panic subsided, she became aware of the stinging on her back where the fence had raked her, a throbbing left paw, and bits of bark and moss stuck to her fur.

She squinted, trying to make out the shapes of her family lying in the bushes. Finally, she saw her mother, Gree, raise her head at her approach, and Pica's terror was suddenly replaced with a wave of relief. She stopped, breathing hard. The relief gave way to shame. She had been incredibly stupid to venture out of their home territory, and even more stupid to enter the construction site. She had completely ignored her parents' rules and had risked her life. She found herself desperately wanting her mother but also fearing her anger.

Dane raised his head and looked at her. A few seconds later, he jumped to his feet and trotted toward her. His smile disappeared as he drew closer, seeing the gash on her side and the way she favoured her front paw.

"Pica — what happened to you?" he questioned. Pica saw all the other heads pop up at his tone, and soon everyone was gathered around her.

"You're hurt!" Gree said with a surprised whine. She quickly inspected Pica's side, finding the wound open and bleeding, and began to lick it clean.

The family clustered around, eyes curious.

"Whoa — what happened to your face?" Kai said with a laugh. "You got brambles stuck all over and —"

"You left the hillside!" her father interrupted with a growl.

Gree stopped licking, exchanging looks with Lamar. "What happened, Pica?" she asked, looking into her daughter's eyes with a mixture of concern and displeasure.

Pica desperately wanted to be somewhere else, feeling hot and uncomfortable with six sets of eyes staring at her. As she told her story, her siblings' eyes grew wider and her parents' and Taba's eyes grew angrier. She hurried through the part where she was trapped inside the fence, and decided to entirely skip the part where she met Scruff and smelled Jagger. As she finished, she returned to her main point: "And I know I shouldn't have gone there, but you have to listen to me — there is a huge building — it's bigger than —"

"Pica!" Gree cut her off, now furious. "You deliberately disobeyed us! Not just in leaving our territory, but in going to see the machines, where we expressly forbid you to go! You put yourself in danger for no reason and you got hurt!"

Pica looked down at the ground, unable to speak out of frustration. She knew her mother was right — she had disobeyed them. But why wouldn't they listen to her warning? "I know, and I'm sorry. But —"

"But nothing," Lamar broke in with a low growl. "You acted selfishly and without thinking. You put us all in danger. And for what? To satisfy your curiosity? I am ashamed of you."

Pica's insides shrivelled and she dropped her belly to the ground, ears back. She couldn't make eye contact.

"Taba, go back to the den site with her," Gree instructed.

Pica crawled away, her tail tucked between her legs. She felt shame burning through her whole body. She winced in pain as she squeezed under a dark, dense bush.

She heard Taba behind her, and felt her rough tongue begin to gently clean up the blood on her side.

"It's okay, Pica," whispered Taba. "Everyone makes mistakes. I know you didn't mean to put us in danger."

Pica looked at her without speaking. What could she say? She felt like no one in her family understood or shared her concern about the construction site. Worse, she didn't get the chance to finish her conversation with Scruff. Why did he suddenly hate her family so much? She sighed. At this point, everything in her life seemed to be going wrong. Her side hurt, she couldn't hunt, she couldn't control her impulses, and every time she thought that things were getting better, she seemed to make another mistake. She closed her eyes and let her head fall heavily onto her front paws. Giving in to the weight of her sadness, she let her body lie still while Taba did her best to clean her wound.

EIGHT
ATTACK

Pica

When it was time to go hunting that night, Gree decided that Dane and Taba would stay behind with Pica so she could rest. Pica's side was already feeling better, but she didn't want to argue with her mother. Shortly after the others had left, Dane and Taba decided to go to the golf course to hunt. "Pica," Taba reminded, "stay here and take it easy. Make sure you're resting your injury. Call if you need anything — we will be close by."

Pica nodded, and watched Dane and Taba dash down the hill. Their shadows faded into the darkness, and then she was alone. She lay there for a while, feeling hungry. She began thinking about her hunting skills. The past few weeks, every time she had been hunting, she had felt the weight of her family watching her, worrying about her. Would she ever improve, and if not, when would they stop helping her? What would happen in the winter when food was harder to find?

Suddenly, a thought made her lift her head. What if it was the stress, not the poor vision, that was stopping her from hunting well? Of course, it probably was her bad eye. But it didn't affect her in other ways anymore — she barely noticed it now. Maybe it would help to hunt alone without anyone watching and judging her. She tilted her head, considering. This could be her opportunity. She had never before been so alone, where no one would wander by to watch and judge her efforts. With a sigh, she reminded herself that she had already gotten into enough trouble for the month. She didn't need to take any more risks. She turned over and curled up tighter. But she couldn't stop wondering. She no longer felt sleepy.

A few minutes later, she gave up trying to convince herself to stay, and rose to her feet. She shouldn't have to go too far — there was the possibility of finding a rodent just uphill from the den site, and up there she wouldn't run into Taba and Dane.

Decision made, Pica trotted quickly uphill, stopping frequently to sniff for danger. At the edge of a patch of particularly sweet grass, she slowed, beginning the hunt. Approaching a large clump of bushes, she smelled the familiar odours of rabbit, vole, and mouse. Her steps became velvety, her small form a shadow. Listening carefully, she began to pick out the small shuffles and chewing of the animals.

Creeping closer, everything stilled around her. The smell of vole got stronger and stronger, and she pushed out all of the other sounds and smells in order to focus on the target. Her mind calmed in a way that she had never before experienced. Her body no longer existed — her mind hovered in the darkness, alert. For the first time, she felt herself become a part of the night.

In front of her, a fat vole emerged from the bush. She could barely see it, but rather sensed its position through a combination of sight, smell, and sound. Teeth chomped on grass, the chewing noise loud in the still night. Pica stopped breathing, completely still now.

In the far corner of her brain, something pushed in, calling for her attention. She frowned and pushed it away — this was always her problem — other thoughts pushing their way in and distracting her. She refocused on the vole. She heard it take a few more steps toward her — now it was within pouncing range. Without thinking, she effortlessly sprung up, spreading her claws. The vole sensed danger, plunging desperately to the side. Pica was also quick in her reaction, shifting her paws as she landed, pinning the vole beneath them. She killed it with a quick shake of her jaws.

For a moment she stood there, the vole hanging from her mouth, dazed. Her whole body felt numb — she couldn't process the fact that she had killed her first healthy, normal prey. Then she grinned and began to savour the taste in her mouth. Relief washed over her as she realized what this meant — she wasn't missing some vital part of herself. She would be able to practise, get better, and be able to rely on herself for food. Maybe she would even be able to start her own pack …

Her reverie was cut short by an alarm sounding in her head. The small something that had been calling for her attention earlier was much louder now. She suddenly became aware of a strong, sour smell. She whipped her head up to see a tall, thin coyote slinking out from behind the bush. He stared at her unblinkingly with glowing, hard, yellow eyes. Breathing in, she recognized his smell — it was Jagger. She had never been this close to him before.

"Nice catch." His voice was quiet, but something about it sent chills through her skin. The fur on her shoulders bristled unconsciously. Dropping the vole in front of her, she backed away a few steps and crouched down.

"You aren't leaving before we've had a chance to get to know one another?" he said in the same odd, calm tone.

Pica stopped her retreat, standing up a little bit straighter. At this point, she knew Dane and Taba were too far away to come immediately. She would have to try to bluff her way out.

"He-hello. I was just hunting. I can leave you the vole if you want, but you should probably move on — this is our home territory." Her voice squeaked awkwardly, not coming out as confidently as she had been hoping.

He didn't reply immediately, continuing to stare at her with narrow, hard eyes. She noticed how long his legs were, his head towering over her. He sized her up with his eyes, and she became acutely aware of her chubby puppy stomach, oversized paws, and short legs. Then, he curled his lips back and showed her his teeth. Pica crouched submissively, her body betraying her. Her tail and ears plastered themselves flat against her head. In a split second, all bravado was gone. She knew instinctively that she was in serious danger, and that she needed help. Raising her head, she howled a high, desperate call. Jagger narrowed his eyes and growled at her. "You've done nothing to deserve this home. Nothing."

At the last word, the tall coyote's muscles bunched up, suddenly visible under his patchy, thin fur, and Pica gasped as she recognized that he was about to spring. Before she could move, he leapt toward her. She saw a dark tower of fur descend and felt the impact, then a sharp pain in her right ear. Letting out a series of sharp yelps, she rolled and tried to get away, but her ear was firmly lodged in his jaws. She was stuck. Her yelping increased in volume as she began to panic, attempting to use her small paws to push and claw at his side. Because he was so much larger than her, she was unable to get a good position, and she felt herself clawing at the air.

Without letting go of her ear, he changed position on top of her and began to claw her side and back, his sharp claws raking through her fur and tearing her skin. He shifted again, and she panicked, knowing he was going to try to go for her stomach. Then, she saw his paw beside her head, and seizing what might be her only opportunity, she turned her head to nip hard at his paw with her sharp baby teeth. She heard a grunt of surprise and felt him momentarily release her ear. Finding herself free, she spurted forward, trying to get out of his way, feeling his teeth brush her back leg as she cleared a low bush and headed downhill toward the den site.

Lowering her head, she stretched her stride out, digging into the earth with her claws. She felt something brush her tail and realized that he was right behind her, within striking distance. Her paw rolled into a dip in the ground and she tumbled, somersaulting down the hill. A shot of pain radiated up her leg, and she yelped in pain and surprise. Jumping up, she readied herself for the impact, but was surprised to see three grey shapes rolling around and onto each other, a chorus of snarls and barks puncturing the air. It was Taba and Dane — they had come!

Pica stepped forward to join them, and the sharp pain shot through her front leg again, from her knee all the way up to her shoulder. She gasped and fell to the ground. She watched helplessly as Dane and Taba worked together to drive Jagger back. She saw Dane's puppy teeth dig into his hind leg as Taba kept his head busy snapping from side to side as she dove quickly in and out. She heard Jagger yelp in pain, and then he shook them off and jumped back.

There was a standoff as the coyotes stared at each other, circling slowly. Taba gave a low, fierce growl. "Get. Out."

Jagger sneered. "Fine. But this won't be the last time you see me." He turned and slowly walked away, not bothering to look behind him. Pica, Dane, and Taba stood in silence, not moving, until his grey shape faded into the darkness. Then Taba turned her head to look at Pica.

"You! What were you thinking?"

Pica lowered her head. There was nothing she could say.

"You're going straight back to the den and you'll stay there until Mom gets back." Taba's voice was very angry. She turned and headed back downhill toward the den.

Dane turned after her and Pica tried to follow. She hopped along, trying not to put any weight on her bad leg, until she stepped into a small depression and stumbled, reflexively putting her leg down to brace herself. She cried out in pain. Dane and Taba turned their heads sharply.

They stared at her as she tucked her leg up tight against her chest, continuing to hobble toward them. She tried not to make eye contact. Their eyes burned into her anyway.

Taba spoke first, a slow exhale. "Oh no." She didn't say anything else. She didn't have to. Pica knew exactly what she was thinking. They all did. An injured leg was a very serious problem, and in some cases a death sentence. If she couldn't use her leg, she would never learn to hunt. If she couldn't hunt, she would probably die.

They waited for her as she slowly hobbled up to them. Then, one on either side, they escorted her back to the den, where she lay down with relief, her whole body shaking with the effort. As she lay in the dirt, she felt Taba's tongue begin to lick her back, and the stinging reminded her that she had wounds there, too. Dane lay beside her, his large brown eyes staring at her with concern. They waited, knowing the others were on their way back and would arrive soon.

NINE
TOGETHER

Scruff

Scruff smelled the blood right away. As he padded through the abandoned lot toward the porch, a tangy, metallic odour hung in the air. Sticking his head under the porch, he saw Jagger lying in the dirt, not moving.

"Jagger! Are you okay?" he pleaded, poking him hard with his nose.

Jagger grunted and lifted his head. He didn't reply immediately, crawling gingerly out from under the porch and standing in the yard to face Scruff. He had cuts and scratches all over him, and he was favouring his back leg. Scruff felt his stomach bunch up in a ball.

"I'm okay. I fought them off." Jagger's voice was pained and angry.

"What happened? Who did this to you?"

"It was that older female pup from the Hillside Pack. And a few of those runts. I was on their side of the fence, but only by a foot or two. I was just passing through, minding my own business, when she jumped out of nowhere and attacked me."

"Why would she do that?"

"Don't you know?" Jagger seemed incredulous.

"They've never attacked us before."

"Think about it. They know we lost our home territory, and they're worried. They want us to move on." He sniffed. "I think she was trying to really hurt me — she jumped on me, trying to get at my neck! Luckily I'm so strong — it was pretty easy to fight her off. But one of the pups got a good bite of my leg."

Scruff took a sharp breath in, wondering which pup it was.

"Did you hurt the pup?"

"Why do you care?" Jagger snapped back. "You care if they live, after what they did to me?"

"No," Scruff replied hastily. "I just wondered what happened, you know, if you got any of them."

There was an uncomfortable silence. Then Jagger continued, "Well, I'm sick of waiting for you to decide what you want to do. It's been more than a week since we talked, and all I get from you is hesitation. I don't think you can delay much longer — they are worried about us, now that our territory is gone. They've gone on the offensive. We need to figure out a plan. It's not safe for us here anymore." He sighed sadly and turned to begin licking his wounds. Scruff padded over and tried to help him, licking some blood off his haunches.

"Ouch — get off of me," Jagger snapped. Then, he softened. "Sorry, it hurts a lot."

Scruff sat down beside him. "What are we going to do about it?"

"Well, we have two options." Jagger paused, looking intently at Scruff. "Either we leave this place and never return. Or, we can stand up for what we deserve, and let them know that they have to let us continue to live here."

Scruff felt panic rise up in his chest. He couldn't imagine leaving this area — it was the only place he had ever known. Also, even though the forest was destroyed, he felt a strong pull to be near it. It was the only link he had to his family. But doing violence to the Hillside Pack — he had been wrestling with this problem for the whole week, and it made him feel sick to think about it. He hated them for killing his mother, but at the same time, he felt a strange draw to Pica and her siblings. He couldn't imagine actually hurting them.

Jagger continued, pushing the point. "Remember, they are monsters. What is going to stop them from continuing? We should stand up to them!"

Scruff hesitated. "I don't know. How are we going to take on such a big pack? They are so much stronger than us. Maybe we should just find somewhere else."

"Fine." Jagger's voice was sarcastic. "We'll just hop over to the next huge peaceful green hillside. I'm sure there is one just down the road, with no coyotes living in it." He paused, and took a deep breath. "Scruff — this is the real world. If we leave, we'll probably have to split up and each find ourselves a sorry little patch of trees that hasn't already been claimed. Is that what you want?"

"No!" Scruff insisted. "I don't want to split up from you. I just don't know how we're going to stand up to such a large pack."

"I have lots of ideas." Jagger grinned, his teeth appearing to glow in the darkness.

"Let me think about it, okay?"

"*Think* about it? Fine! You can think about it while they organize themselves to come and kill us. That's a great idea. I can't deal with you right now. You're so weak sometimes. See you later. Maybe."

Watching his retreating form, Scruff felt the panic rising up in him, stronger now. Dark birds flashed through his mind, circling, circling, waiting to claw his throat out. He didn't want to be alone again. The anger and fear welled up in him, and he raced after Jagger, running up to his side.

"No — don't leave. I'll help you. We can make a plan — talk to Lamar or something. Let's give it a try."

Jagger stopped and gave him a cool smile. "I'm glad you're with me on this one. You know, it's only right. They've stepped over the line. Now we need to show them again where that line is."

"So do you think we should —"

"I have a plan."

"Okay, but I don't want to —"

"Don't worry about it. You won't have to do anything. Just follow me now." Jagger walked away into the darkness without looking back. Despite feeling uncomfortable and scared, Scruff followed him down the alley, across the busy road, and toward the industrial area down by the train tracks. He noticed that Jagger no longer seemed to be favouring his hind leg, and walked confidently, strongly, a dark shadow in the night.

TEN
APART

Pica

Taba kept watch over Pica while Dane tried to make contact with the rest of the pack. It wasn't long before Pica saw Gree and Lamar galloping toward them across the hillside. They pulled up, breathless, and Dane, Kai, and Sage arrived shortly after.

Gree looked at Taba and Pica, panic in her face. Pica got to her feet gingerly, one paw curled up close to her, her head low in shame. Her mother came over and Pica buried her head in Gree's thick fur.

"Ohhh." Gree's voice was half breath, half moan. Taba nodded silently. No one else moved.

"What happened — tell us everything," Lamar demanded.

Dane and Taba both turned to Pica.

She realized that they had no idea about what happened. She looked down at the ground. "Well ..." She stopped, not sure how to continue.

"It's okay," Lamar said, prodding. "I know it was scary. But you have to let us know what happened."

"We came back, and I was lying by the den while Dane and Taba were in the golf course." She saw Lamar and Gree look sharply at Taba, but they did not interrupt. She took a deep breath and then continued, "I wanted to see if I could hunt on my own, without anyone watching me, so I went over to the bushes by the path over there. I caught a vole, and then Jagger was there. He was on our territory, and attacked me. I called for them and they helped to fight him off."

Dane picked up the story. "We heard her howl for help and raced over. He was already on top of her. Taba jumped on him and we all drove him away, but not before he had the chance to injure her."

Taba looked up, adding, "We did the best we could. But I don't think he's gone for long."

There was a stunned silence as the rest of the pack took in the information.

"I'll kill him." Lamar broke the silence angrily. "This time, he has gone too far. This is a call to war."

Pica was surprised that he wasn't mad at her for straying from the others. Instead, he seemed furious that Jagger would enter into their territory at all.

Gree looked at him, many different emotions flying over her face. "Lamar. Let's think carefully about how to respond. If you go in there on your own, you could get hurt, too."

"He's smaller than I am, and besides, if you come with me, you leave Taba and the pups undefended. That is too dangerous right now. Who knows — what if he gets past me and circles back?"

Gree sighed. "I don't know. Don't forget that he's got that pup with him. Maybe we should wait —"

"I have no choice — if I don't follow him now, we'll appear weak. And if we don't know when he will strike next, we'll have to be on guard at all times, and stay together. Don't worry about that runt — I could take him out with a swipe. Gree, you know we can't wait on this one."

Gree acquiesced, reluctance in her voice. "Well, we have to do something. Try to take him by surprise, attack him, and make your point. But get away quickly. You don't have to kill him to make yourself heard." She paused, adding, "Just be careful to watch for that pup, too."

"I will," Lamar assured her. "You know, this isn't the first time that a coyote has tried to challenge our territory. I'll deal with it the way I always do." He walked over and nosed her neck gently. She sighed.

"I know. I just wish I could go with you this time. Be careful."

"I will."

Pica glanced at Dane, hoping to make eye contact. He looked as tense and anxious as she felt, and didn't look away from Lamar.

"All right," Gree announced, the final decision made. "Track him now, while his scent is still fresh. Be careful — it will be light soon. If you don't find him before daybreak, return here and we'll regroup. I love you. Don't take any risks — we can't afford another injury."

Pica clamped her mouth shut to stop herself from crying out. She didn't want her father to leave. She had looked into Jagger's eyes, and what she saw scared her. She also worried about Scruff — would he get hurt in this, too? But now the events were set into motion, Lamar already galloping off across the hillside. They watched his shadow disappear into the darkness. All the coyotes slowly found a spot to lie down, their heads still oriented toward the departing shadow, and settled in for a tense wait.

Pica's mind raced. If she hadn't left the den site to try hunting on her own, she would never have been in a situation where she could be attacked. She knew that Jagger shouldn't have been on their territory, but couldn't help feeling guilty for her part in this. How many times had her parents reminded the pups to always stay close, so that they could help to drive other coyotes off their territory? She had seen this many times before — a coyote would accidentally stray onto their territory, and either Gree or Lamar would bark or run at them, warning them to move on. And they always did. But last night, she had been all on her own, with no help close by.

She glanced over at Dane, and caught him staring at her with a worried expression. Guilt and shame coursed through her body. If only she hadn't been so selfish, she would have thought about the danger she was putting her whole family in. The fact that she had caught her first prey was completely overshadowed by the rest of the evening.

She turned away. She couldn't bear to look into his eyes. She repositioned herself into a ball and closed her eyes, trying to block out the pain throbbing up her leg and along her back and side.

ELEVEN

LEAP

Scruff

Scruff loped behind Jagger, following him to the far edge of the housing subdivision, away from the hillside. Jagger stopped more frequently than usual to mark poles and bushes. Scruff wondered why he wanted their track to be so obvious. The older coyote didn't hesitate, but seemed to know exactly where he was going. Everything was dark and still. Other than the sound of their paws on the pavement, Scruff heard nothing.

On the other side of the busy road was an area with larger buildings. They didn't typically go through this area because there was very little food available — fewer green spaces where rodents liked to live, and the garbage bins were mostly well secured. In addition, during the day, the place was crawling with humans. Now, though, in the very early hours of the morning before first light, it was quiet and still.

They rounded the corner of one of the tall buildings, and on the other side Scruff saw a gap where a building should be. Instead, there was a gaping hole in the ground and lots of machinery. Another construction site. Jagger threaded his way through the equipment, ducking under the fence where it had begun to sag out. He walked carefully along the edge of the pit. Scruff, shadowing him, looked down into the gaping hole and gasped. It seemed to go down forever, dark walls descending into even more darkness. At the bottom, he saw what might be some construction equipment, although in the darkness they looked like hulking shadows of giant animals. Jagger stepped back from the pit and settled down beside the base of a large machine, licking the dirt out from between the pads of his paws.

"All right." He looked up at Scruff. "Here's the plan. You stay here. Don't make a sound, and don't move. No matter what. Understand?"

"But what —"

"You don't need to know anything else. Just shut your mouth and do as I tell you."

The sharp tone and look in his eyes silenced Scruff. He had no idea what Jagger was planning, and it felt dangerous to ask, given his current mood. Jagger exited the construction site without a backward glance, heading back in the direction of the housing subdivision. Scruff stood up and took a few steps as if to follow him, then thought better of it. Jagger could be very cruel when his orders weren't followed. He decided to stay put and think it through.

Everything was still and silent, except for an occasional breeze that ruffled some of the plastic that covered a big pile. He shivered a little bit, although not entirely from the cold. He felt nervous and very much awake, his brain working hard to figure out where Jagger might have gone and why he had been told to stay here.

Almost an hour passed, and Scruff decided that it was a bad idea to stay. Whatever Jagger was planning, he owed it to Scruff to tell him more about it. If they were going to be in a pack together, it needed to be more equal. With a sigh, he stood up and began to walk toward the fence. Suddenly he heard the sound of swift running, pads scraping on gravel. He saw Jagger slip under the fence and head straight toward him at a full gallop.

"Jagger! What —"

Scruff didn't get another syllable out before Jagger leapt on top of him, and he felt sharp teeth bite into the flesh of his ear. Jagger had punished him before for being stupid or careless, but this time seemed much rougher. He yelped loudly, crying out in pain and surprise — was Jagger mad because he had moved from the original spot where he had been told to stay? He desperately tried to drag himself away, crying out, "Jagger! Stop! You're hurting me!"

Jagger shook his head roughly, flipping Scruff over and taking some flesh out of his ear as he went. The hot burning caused Scruff to panic, and he began to yelp uncontrollably, crying out loudly and turning onto his back, paws up.

"Please! Why are you doing this? Stop!"

Suddenly, there was nothing. Jagger had disappeared. Scruff looked around from his position on the ground, afraid to get up. He continued his keening wail, crying out the pain and sadness. Why had Jagger turned on him like that? What had he done wrong? He flipped back onto his belly, and kept his head on the ground, his ears back. He whimpered a little bit more, looking around for Jagger.

Then he saw another dark shape slip under the fence and drift toward him. He cowered, squinting to see who it was. It wasn't Jagger. His relief was cut short when he saw who it was — Lamar.

He jumped to his feet now, tail up. There was no sign of Jagger, who, despite being cruel, was his only hope at this point. The situation had suddenly gone from bad to worse. He took a step backwards, and then another one. Lamar continued walking toward him threateningly, his tail high in the air and his ears back. He gave a low growl. With the next step back, Scruff felt nothing but air. He risked a quick glance backwards and gasped, realizing that he was right at the edge of the pit. Another step back and he would fall in. He froze, unable to move.

Lamar kept approaching until he was a few metres from Scruff, and then stopped. His ears swivelled from side to side, and he sniffed the air. He seemed confused. "What's going on — where's Jagger? Who attacked you?"

Scruff was silent. He didn't want to tell the truth, because despite the attack, he still felt a sense of loyalty to

Jagger. But his mind had gone blank — he couldn't think of a lie that would make sense.

Lamar took a few more steps toward him, cocking his head to the side. Then, out of the darkness, a shadow surged toward them. Scruff saw Lamar's confusion turn to horror as he realized that Jagger's powerful body was about to collide with him. Before Lamar could react, Jagger hit him hard, causing him to lose his balance and skid toward the edge of the pit. Scruff heard him cry out in terror, his claws scrabbling against the earth as he tried to regain his balance. His hind legs slipped off the edge, and with a terrible howl, he disappeared. There was a brief silence followed by a dull thud that echoed off the dirt walls. Scruff was unable to move, in complete shock. All he could hear was his own ragged breath.

Jagger walked slowly to the edge and looked over. Scruff stared at him, his eyes wide. Then Jagger turned back to him with a wide smile, his teeth gleaming in the darkness. "He's dead. Come and see."

Trembling, Scruff turned and took a few steps to stand by Jagger's side. He peered down into the darkness. A shadowy form was lying at the bottom of the pit, legs splayed at odd angles. Nothing moved. There was no way a coyote could survive a fall like that. Scruff felt suddenly nauseous, and his stomach heaved. Jagger made a move toward him, and he stiffened, thinking the larger coyote was about to push him over, too. But Jagger just touched him gently with his nose and gave him a nod of approval. "Good work."

Scruff stared at him, realizing slowly that this had been the plan all along. Jagger had lied to Scruff, using him to distract Lamar so that he could take him by surprise. Scruff felt his stomach knotting. He looked away from Jagger quickly, staring down into the dark pit. If Jagger knew how horrified he was about this, he might turn on Scruff. He tried to steady his breathing and appear normal.

Scruff knew he needed to say something. "Thanks," he attempted. It came out as a squeak. He tried again. "Did you plan that, the whole thing?" He tried to sound admiring.

"Yes. But if I told you, you wouldn't have cried so convincingly. Sorry I had to hurt you."

"It's okay. I'll be okay."

"I couldn't have done it without you."

Scruff didn't reply. Even yesterday, these words would have meant a lot to him. But now, he couldn't help but feel that he was standing next to someone he didn't know at all. He needed to get away from Jagger and get some space to think.

"So ... what's next?" he asked.

"You'll find out," Jagger replied, grinning. "Let's go."

He turned and trotted back toward the housing subdivision. Scruff turned and followed him slowly, his mind working on ways to get away without Jagger realizing why.

"I'm a little hungry. I think I'll just do a bit of hunting on the way home," he ventured.

Jagger stopped and turned to look at him, his eyes suspicious.

"We can hunt together on the way," he replied, with a note of finality.

Scruff decided to go along with it for the moment, and to try to find out more about his plan. As they trotted together, his thoughts raced. If Jagger had lied about this, what else had he lied about? Why had he really adopted Scruff? He immediately thought of Pica's family. Was it true? Had they killed his parents? He suddenly realized that he didn't know who to trust anymore. He had a sudden, compelling need to find Pica and warn her. Even if her family was awful, he didn't want anything to happen to her. He had to figure out how to get away. He took a shaky breath, and trotted off after Jagger.

TWELVE
STILLNESS

Pica

The hillside coyote family waited through the darkness until the night began to think about becoming day. It was almost unbearable, but Pica didn't want to make it worse for her mother by saying anything. Besides, she couldn't think clearly with her body throbbing. Each moment was agony — either she was aware of her own physical pain, or she was thinking about how this whole problem was mostly her fault. If she hadn't gone to the construction site in the first place and injured herself, she wouldn't have had to stay back from the hunt. And if she hadn't left the den site to try hunting on her own, Jagger wouldn't have found her alone.

"It wasn't your fault." Her mother was lying next to her, and spoke gently as if she could read her thoughts.

"I'm sorry," was all Pica could say in reply.

"Jagger has a history of aggression, and if it wasn't this time it would have been another. We should have driven him away long ago. We took chances we shouldn't have."

Sage raised her head. "I'm glad that we aren't like that."

"You can't be too nice, though," argued Kai. "You see what can happen? I agree with Mom. We should have done something a long time ago." He was angry.

"Well, it's not easy to know the future," Gree replied. "We can't go around injuring every coyote who makes a play for our land. Coyotes come through all the time hoping to hunt near our den site, and if we went after all of them we would all end up with leg injuries." She looked at Pica and licked the side of her face lovingly. "It's all about reading their body language and trusting your gut instinct. Most of them move on easily as soon as you stand up for yourself, and never give it a second thought. We made a mistake with Jagger. He didn't follow the code, and we misread the situation."

"What code?" Sage asked.

"When a coyote wants to challenge for land, he or she will approach the head of the pack that lives there and challenge them. It is direct and face to face. They battle it out to decide who is stronger, fitter, and more deserving."

"To the death?" Kai breathed.

"No, not often. Usually, after a few moments, it is clear who the fitter coyote is, and the other one submits."

"Have you fought like that?" Pica asked. She was very interested — her mother had never talked to them about this before. She had seen them both stand up to coyotes who were passing through the territory, but never in her lifetime had she seen it come to a physical confrontation.

"Yes. A few times. But it never went very far."

They were all silent for a while, thinking about Jagger, and how different this new confrontation was. The sky continued to lighten and there was still no sign of Lamar.

Scruff

It was dawn before Jagger fell into a sound sleep. As promised, he had helped Scruff to hunt, finding and killing a young, injured raccoon. As they feasted on it, rather than making his stomach feel better, tearing into the flesh made Scruff feel even sicker. He found it difficult to meet Jagger's eyes. He kept thinking back to Lamar's body dropping away from him, into the darkness.

After they had eaten, they went back under the porch of the abandoned house. Scruff attempted to talk to Jagger.

"So, what are you going to do now?"

Jagger looked at him sharply. "Don't you mean, what are *we* going to do? Or have you lost your courage, runt?"

"Sorry. What are we going to do now?" Scruff hoped to sound convincing.

"You'll find out in the morning." Jagger's teeth glinted white as he grinned. He scratched the dirt, turned a couple of times, and flopped down. Scruff stared at his back, angry. Jagger was acting like he was the only one who mattered, and Scruff was nothing to him. Scruff wondered again why Jagger had adopted him in the first place. He was now too afraid of the larger coyote to ask.

Scruff waited until he was sure that Jagger was fully asleep. He saw the large paws twitching and heard the low, deep breathing. Slowly, carefully, he got up and left the porch. As he reached the edge of the property, he glanced back at the hulking form lying under the porch. It didn't move. He padded softly down the alley, got to the fenceline, pushed through, and walked slowly down the hillside toward the den site. A deep sense of guilt and dread gnawed at him. He didn't know why he felt the need to warn Pica's family, but somehow his body kept moving in their direction.

In the dim light, he saw a cluster of grey shapes in the grass. He heard Gree's warning bark and they stood then, tails and hackles raised aggressively. He saw one shape still on the ground — Pica. That was odd. Was she injured? He continued on down the hill slowly, unsure of why he was there. Why did he feel the need to help this family ... who had never helped him? He stopped a few feet from them, facing six pairs of hard, angry eyes. He looked down. Then Gree gave a low, threatening growl that broke the silence.

"What?" She could barely get the syllable out.

He swallowed. Then he said it all in a single, quick breath. "Jagger killed Lamar and now I think he is going to come after you."

The words hung in the air, overinflated, blocking everything else out. It was as if someone had hit pause on the scene, bodies frozen in shock. Then, a long in-take of breath, and a slow, keening wail. Gree threw her head back and cried out. The wail was high and thin, and sounded harsh in the early morning quiet. Then, Taba joined in, and the pups, too. Scruff bent his head down low, buffeted by the pain and the sadness contained in the chorus. The cry continued for about thirty seconds, and then trailed off.

"You." Gree stared at him with such a deep hatred. "You helped him." It was not a question.

"I ... I didn't mean to ... well ... I guess I did," Scruff stammered. He glanced quickly at Pica. Her large, brown eyes registered horror, and he looked quickly away. He started again, trying to explain the situation. "Last night, well —"

"I don't care what excuses you have." Gree spoke bitterly. "Tell us what you came to tell us, and then get away from me."

Scruff spoke quickly and urgently. "He won't tell me what his plan is, but I know Jagger wants this hillside. I think he is prepared to do anything to get it. He killed Lamar last night, and —" He paused as he saw Gree flinch with pain at the mention of Lamar. He breathed out, and started again, "— and I'm pretty sure that he is going to continue with some kind of aggression. I don't know what he is planning."

Gree looked at him for a few moments, her eyes burning with anger. "Thank you." She spat out the words. "Now go."

Taba growled, and took a threatening step toward Scruff.

"I'm sorry." He didn't know what else to say. Lamar's body falling flashed through his vision again. Taba growled again, more aggressively this time.

Gree shook her head. "You will never be welcome anywhere near us. If you ever come near us again, I will rip your throat out."

He looked down the line of coyotes. They all stared at him with hatred. He took one last glance at Pica. She looked like she was in shock. Scruff knew he had no choice. He turned and galloped away. He could barely feel his feet on the ground as he headed through the golf course and across the road. He didn't know where he was going, but knew he had to get far, far away so that Jagger wouldn't be able to find him. He wondered what the Hillside Pack would do. Would they stay and fight? Would they flee? His breath came hard and fast as he pushed faster and faster, following a railway track, not bothering to even look at his surroundings. For the first time since he was born, he was truly alone in the world.

Gree

After Scruff left, Gree concentrated on breathing steadily, trying to calm herself and figure out what to do. She looked at her children, who all looked to her for guidance, fear in their eyes. She felt numb, as if a part of her had been ripped out. Lamar was dead. She couldn't believe it. She felt terrible, knowing that she hadn't done more to dissuade Lamar from trying to take on Jagger. They should have known how dangerous it would be.

She weighed her options. If they stayed to fight, only she and Taba were strong enough to stand up to Jagger. They stood a good chance, two on one. However, Jagger hadn't been attacking in the usual, direct way. He was sneaky. He could wait until they had to split up to get food, and pick off one of her pups, or Taba. Even her — she was strong, but she was still smaller than Jagger. And then there was Pica. She glanced at her daughter, who had lain back down, obviously in a lot of pain. She couldn't hunt, and couldn't keep up with them. When everyone got hungry, they would have to leave her behind, alone, to go hunt. She couldn't bear the thought of losing another from their pack. They had to leave the hillside — it was the only way she could see to avoid losing another life.

"Okay." She turned to look at her children. "We have to go; otherwise we'll be in danger. We can't stick together all of the time, and Jagger will do what he did with Pica, find one of us alone and attack us."

"But Mom!" Dane protested. "We can't just give up."

"We aren't. In the spring, when you and the others are bigger, we can come back and challenge him. We just have to find somewhere to survive the winter."

They were all quiet, thinking. Although none of them wanted to leave their home, they knew that what she said made sense. "We have to leave now, because Pica is going to be slow. We need to get her somewhere where she can recover safely."

Pica looked up at her mother and nodded. "I understand."

"Okay. We leave now." Gree turned toward the road and began walking slowly. The others formed a line behind her, Taba taking the rear behind the limping Pica. Gree resisted the urge to look behind her. She didn't want to have to see the first rays of the early morning light casting a glow across the hillside. Her home was gone, and she needed to use all of her energy to make sure that they found a safe place to stay until they could regroup and help Pica get better.

THIRTEEN
SCHOOL

Pica

The Hillside Pack travelled through the dawn and, as the sun slowly rose in the sky, tried to get some distance from the golf course. Rain pelted them, trickling through Pica's thick fur and sliding down the sides of her face. They couldn't travel quickly because Pica had to hop along, her good front leg tiring more with every step. She felt cold and then hot, shivering as she walked.

Pica was barely aware of where they were going, but she knew they were farther than she had ever been before. At one point, they were in an area with lots of low buildings. Trucks came and went along the front the buildings, so they headed around back, where it was quieter. Pica saw a dirt patch behind a Dumpster and flopped down with a groan. She felt the wet concrete soaking her fur. The others lay down, too, resting quietly next to her, licking the dirt out of their paws.

"Mom — we can't just let him drive us away!" Kai broke the silence.

"We have no choice." Gree looked off into the air beside him, not making eye contact with the pups. She seemed distant, and Pica knew that she was still reeling after the death of Lamar.

"But it's our home! And there are six of us!" Kai was becoming hysterical.

"We have no choice," Gree repeated.

"But he killed Dad! We can't just let him have our land. We have to fight him."

"Shut up, Kai!" barked Dane. "Stop it. It's not like any of us wanted to leave."

Gree looked at them. Her expression looked broken as she tried to compose herself. "It's okay. I'm angry, too. I know it hurts to just leave like that, but he is larger than any one of us right now. We risk a lot by attacking him. I've already lost enough ..." Her voice broke and she took a short breath before continuing, "I refuse to lose anyone else." She paused, taking another, deeper breath. "It's not forever. But we have to wait until you are all bigger and stronger. We can return and take it back — but not now."

Kai was silent, his face angry. Pica understood his feelings. She felt a rage, white-hot in her belly, wanting nothing more than to tear Jagger and Scruff to pieces. But she was still small, and so were her siblings. And although Gree was an excellent hunter and very smart, she simply didn't have the same mass and muscle as Jagger did. If they all coordinated an attack, they might have a chance, but it was far more likely that one of them would be injured and Jagger would escape.

They lay in silence for hours as the rain tapered off. Pica looked over at Gree, who lay still, staring at the side of a building. A few moments later, Gree rolled to her stomach and stood up, stretching. "We should keep moving. I don't think Jagger is coming after us, but I still want to put some more distance between us. We need to find some food, too."

They continued on through the grey afternoon, sticking to areas without many humans or cars. At the edge of the industrial buildings, they found train tracks, and followed those for a while. Pica's good leg was getting so tired that pains began to shoot up toward her shoulder. One of her leg muscles twitched and then cramped up. She tried to put some weight on her bad leg, but cried out as she remembered why she was holding it up. The ground around her swam, and she almost lost her balance. Taking a deep breath, she forced herself to keep going. Sage looked over at her with concern.

"Where are we going?" she heard Sage ask Gree.

"I don't know yet," Gree answered. "We need to find somewhere safe to sleep, with food nearby."

Despite the gravity of the situation, Pica's siblings couldn't help having fun. They tried balancing on the railway and jumping the crossties. She watched Kai's face, deep in concentration, as he teetered on the track. All four paws were in a line, claws out but of no help on the slippery metal. He took a tentative step forward, then another.

"Hey, I'm finally —" he began, but then all four paws jumped in the air and he fell off, an expression of surprise on his face. "Hey!" He cocked his head to the side. "It's rumbling!" he yelped. "What does that mean?"

"A train is coming." Gree was serious. "Everyone, get away from the tracks. In those bushes, there." She indicated some bushes in the deep ditch at the side of the tracks. Sage leapt first, a small squeak of fear escaping her. The others quickly followed. Pica found the spot next to her. She could feel her sister's body shaking.

The rumbling feeling intensified, and with it the sound of something big approaching. It got louder and louder, until it seemed like it couldn't get any more intense. Then, wind blew back the bushes, smacking them in their faces, and there was a piercing horn that seemed to poke fire into her ears. A bright light shone so hard into their eyes that they shut them to stop the pain. Pica yelped in panic, closing her eyes and flattening her body against the earth. She pressed against Sage, unable to think. The sound continued for a long time. Eventually, she felt brave enough to crack her eyes open and watch the giant metal cars go past. When it was finally over, they all stared at the back of the train, smoothly moving away from them along the track.

"Whoa." Dane was the first to be able to speak. Pica smiled at him. Now that it had passed, she wanted to see it again. She had never seen anything that powerful or loud before. She forgot her pain for a moment, soaking in the power of the machine.

"That was cool!" Kai exclaimed. "Can we stay here? I think Sage would love to see another one!" He bumped into her with his body, poking fun at her still-traumatized expression. She snapped out of it, pushing him back with all her force.

"Be quiet, Kai. Let's just keep going."

"Good idea, Sage." Gree smiled in agreement.

While they were travelling, Pica watched Gree sniff very carefully whenever they encountered a large patch of bushes or a tree, to find out what coyotes had passed through and if any lived there. A few times they had to leave the train tracks to go around someone's home territory, but they always came back to the tracks after. Eventually, the land around them began to get busier with buildings, and they stopped in the shelter of a bush to wait for nightfall. Pica was relieved. She didn't know how much farther she could go. She closed her eyes and fell into a deep stupor.

The cold woke her up. She opened one eye, noticing that the sky had gone dark. She shivered hard — her fur was still wet, and the night breeze filtered under the shelter of the bush. She squirmed closer to the warm body behind her — it was Taba. She looked around sleepily. "Hey — where's everyone else?"

"Not far," Taba spoke gently. "Just sleep for now. Mom is looking for a place where we can stay awhile, somewhere safe for you to get better. They will come back and get us soon."

Pica started to protest, but felt so exhausted and cold that she decided to curl up a little closer to Taba and wait.

The next time she opened her eyes, it was in response to her mother's insistent licks.

"Pica." Gree's voice was concerned. "You okay?"

"I think so." Pica shook her head a little bit to try to clear her head. "Did you find somewhere for us to go?"

"Yes. We found a spot nearby. It isn't far, and you should be able to make it."

Pica rose to her feet. She was surprised at how shaky her legs felt. She felt suddenly very hot, and every muscle ached. She tried to hide it by taking a breath in and heading straight. When she stumbled on a root, though, she could tell her mother noticed. Coming to her side, Gree leaned gently into her. Pica felt the warm body breathing next to her, and it gave her some extra energy.

"You can do it," Gree whispered softly to her. "You have to."

As her mother headed off slowly, Pica followed her, just trying to keep her tail in sight and step where she stepped. Her siblings all ran on ahead. After a couple of hours, with lots of breaks, they arrived at the entrance to a park. Two large cedar trees marked the entrance, which was about one city block square. Limping slowly into the park, she smelled water and headed straight for a small stream that ran through the middle of it, drinking greedily. She hadn't realized how thirsty she was. After sating her thirst, she sat down in the grass and closed her eyes.

A meaty smell woke her, and she opened her eyes to see a fresh rat in front of her.

"Caught it myself!" Kai said gleefully.

"Thanks." She smiled, and tried to eat it. It was odd — she didn't feel very hungry. Suddenly, mid-chew, she heard Gree's sharp bark, warning them of danger nearby. She jumped to her feet, Kai next to her, and they saw Gree and the others running toward them. Then, from behind her she heard another series of barks. She turned to see coyotes, one larger than any coyote she had ever seen. They were staring at her and Kai with hostility.

"What are you doing here?" the female barked. Before they could respond, their mother was there.

"Excuse us. We'll move on now. Come on, pups, follow me," Gree replied with a sigh. They left the park, and the two coyotes watched them leave, tails and hackles up. "Sorry about that," Gree apologized to them. "I knew that it was someone's home territory, but there was no evidence that they had been here recently. I thought we could get away with it just for a day."

They walked as quickly as Pica could go. The sky was lightening, and they could hear the first few cars of the day start up, coughing to life in the cold morning air. Pica knew they had very little time left to find a spot to sleep.

"What are we going to do now?" Dane asked, worry in his voice.

Gree paused, looking back at them. "Honestly, I don't know. We need to find somewhere quiet to pass the next day. Somewhere close."

Pica looked down. She knew that she was the reason they were in so much trouble. "Maybe I can just find a bush, and you guys can go find somewhere for us to stay.

You could come back tomorrow." She looked longingly at a bush as they passed, the darkness beneath beckoning her.

"We're not leaving you," snapped Gree.

Pica stumbled on, her legs as heavy as lead, her head dropping down. She lost track of where she was as the minutes ticked by. Suddenly, she became aware that they had stopped in a big, empty field. A large building stood on the far side. They stood there for about a minute. Nothing moved. Then, Gree did a quick circuit.

"No one lives here. It's weird — such a perfect spot, I can't understand it ..." Her voice trailed off as she saw Pica's exhausted face. A car turned onto the street they were standing on and passed to the side of them with a roar of blinding lights.

"It's fine for now, anyway," Gree finished.

They found a gap in the fence and headed to the largest clump of bushes, tucked into the side of the field, sheltered by a stand of tall oak trees. Pica sagged to the ground, making it only halfway under the bush, and immediately sank into darkness.

She was only vaguely aware of the passage of time, feeling warm bodies lying next to her, trying to warm her up. Her mother's rough tongue scraped her back, touching wounds that felt like they were on fire. During the day, she felt slightly warmer, but her whole body shook with the cold at night.

It might have been a day, or maybe two or three, when suddenly there were barks and growls, and the sound of lots of people screaming and shouting. She opened her eyes, and saw a cluster of humans — many of them small —

on the far side of the field, standing in a clump and pointing in her direction. Her siblings stood a few feet away, growling at them, standing their ground. She shook her head, suddenly alert.

"Pica — can you come with us?" Gree barked at her sharply. "We have to go — there are too many humans here, and they see us. It isn't safe."

"Mom — I can't." Pica was defeated. She knew she wouldn't be able to travel anymore.

"Pica, come on. We can't leave you here!" Sage yelled at her, running over and burying her nose under Pica's side, pushing to try to help her up.

Pica tried to get to her feet, but her whole body shook and then gave out underneath her. "I'm sorry — I have to stay here. You guys go — maybe they won't notice me." She crawled a little deeper under the bush.

Then, Gree was beside her, nosing her face. "I'm so sorry, but I can't stay with you. I love you. Go deeper into this bush. We'll distract them by running out the side. Don't move, and we'll come back for you tonight."

Pica gave a wry smile at the instructions "don't move." This was finally one time where she would obey her mother. With that, Gree and the rest of her siblings were gone. She heard more barking and shouting, and then everything was quiet. She closed her eyes and let her body relax into sleep again.

FOURTEEN

CITY

Scruff

Leaving the hillside, Scruff was numb. He didn't know where he was going, unable to think about anything other than what had happened over the past day. He headed in a direction that he had never before travelled, moving quickly. He barely felt the freezing rain that soaked his fur. Images of Lamar's body lying at the bottom of the pit haunted his thoughts.

He snapped back to the present as something hissed in front of him. Before he could react, a small black-and-white animal turned its tail toward him and covered him with a thick film of sulphurous poison. There was a moment where Scruff didn't feel anything but surprise, and then his eyes were on fire, his nose seared, his throat filled with the thick gas. He couldn't breathe or see, and as he tried to get away, blinded, he fell into the street and his head hit something hard. He made a high, keening wail as he tried to stand, but hit his head again — he was stuck under something.

For the next little while, he rolled from side to side, moaning and trying to scratch at his eyes. His head pounded and he felt a burning deep inside his chest. Jagger had warned him about skunks, but he had never before experienced this. He cursed himself for not paying more attention. Now he was going to die here, writhing in pain, because of a stupid mistake.

Over time, the pain began to recede, and he became more aware of his surroundings. He was able to open his eyes and see shapes, and he realized he was stuck under a car. Squeezing out from underneath, he stood shakily, his head pounding. It was then that he became aware of the smell. Burning up through his nose and into the back of his throat was an oily, sulphurous odour that blocked out everything else. He turned his head from side to side, unable to sense his surroundings by smell, as he normally did. Even though his eyes were open now, he still felt blind. He trotted slowly down the sidewalk, trying to escape it, but realized with a sinking feeling that it was following him. His fur was coated in the sticky substance.

The sky was beginning to lighten, and humans began to appear on the street. Scruff was miserable: wet, cold, hungry, his paws throbbing. His head pounded from the stench. Rolling on the ground, he tried to scrape it off. That helped a bit, but as he trotted on, he realized he was now completely unable to smell danger or prey. He no longer cared that Jagger might be coming after him — he simply didn't have any energy left. He needed to find somewhere to lie down and get out of the way of the humans for the day. Realizing that he wouldn't be able to tell whether he was in neutral territory or not, he picked a bush at random and curled up underneath it, hoping for the best.

He passed the day sleeping fitfully, waking frequently with images of Lamar's body or the skunk swimming in his vision. When darkness fell again, his stomach rumbled loudly, forcing him to his feet. He set off, knowing he needed to get farther away from the hillside. He tried to find prey as he travelled, but was unable to smell anything other than himself. He resorted to picking through garbage to find food, barely even able to taste it. He found that he didn't have to worry about other coyotes, because no one would go near him.

A few nights passed like this, and, as he continued on, the buildings got bigger and closer together. One night, he stopped at a busy road and realized he could barely even see the sky through all of the tall buildings. He felt an odd sense of relief, knowing he was far away from anyone and anything he had ever known. He doubled back and found a quiet alley, and stood for a moment, listening to the sounds of car tires on wet streets, honking, and people talking. Here, it was noisy even at night.

He began making his way down the alley, no plan in mind. There were cars parked in rows along both sides, leaving a narrow strip of road in the middle. He followed the edge of the buildings until he saw a large, dry area with cars parked in it. He ducked into the dry warmth gratefully, looking around cautiously to make sure there were no other animals or humans. In a corner, there were some tarps and blankets piled behind a car. Suddenly exhausted, he burrowed himself deep under the blankets. Closing his eyes, he fell asleep.

What seemed like moments later, his sleep was interrupted by a shrill wailing noise. Panicked, he raised his head and looked around. The noise seemed to be coming from the other side of the lot. He jumped out of the tarp pile and slunk carefully around the side of the car, peeking out to see what it was. He breathed in as he saw that the dry covered area was filled with humans, getting into their cars, talking, and walking past. It was dawn. He could not believe the sudden transformation. His ears and nose twitched from side to side, trying to take it all in. The piercing noise suddenly stopped, and two humans climbed into one of the cars. Suddenly afraid of being spotted, he crept backwards, retreating toward the blankets. Digging into them again, he realized he was trapped. If he tried to leave now, he would be spotted. He curled up deeper in the blankets, eyes peeking out to see if he could find an escape route.

Then, before he had a plan, two humans were standing right beside his tarp, talking. He turned his head slowly, assessing their distance, and waited, afraid to move another muscle. He heard two sharp beeps, and then they got into the car that was parked in front of the tarps where he lay. With a loud growl, the car started, belching a disgusting smelling smoke all over him. He panicked, his fear of cars magnified by the noise and smell. Jumping up, he left the blanket before the car could run him over. As he ran past the side of the car, he heard screaming and a sharp, painful honk of the horn pierced his eardrums. He ran quickly, trying to put some distance between him and the car, entering the alley and running along it, looking desperately for another place to hide. He saw some bushes behind a Dumpster, and dove into them, shaking. All around him, he heard noises. Humans talking, the banging of doors, radios and music.

He lay there for the next few hours, alert, becoming slowly desensitized to all of the sounds. He began to be able to differentiate between them better. Cars passed through often, but there were long periods with no cars, too. Humans stayed mostly inside the buildings, and their muffled sounds filtered down through windows and onto the street. Occasionally there would be a much louder sound — a siren or a loud truck, but if he flattened his ears to his head, it helped to drown the sound out a little, and it would typically pass quickly.

He had been lying there for several hours, waiting uneasily, when he suddenly became aware of a sniffing noise. He looked in the direction of the noise and saw a wet black nose poking through the bushes, a few feet from his head. He leapt backwards as it began to bark furiously. It leapt into the bushes after him as he exited the far side, running around the side of a Dumpster. He looked back and saw her — wide, floppy ears, a brown colour, and about his height, although a bit heavier. She barked loudly, and although he couldn't understand exactly what she was saying, she sounded aggressive and angry. She began to run at him, and he fled into the alley, moving quickly and passing two humans, who yelled at either him or the dog, he wasn't sure. He turned the corner onto the street.

He stole a glance behind him — the dog was still in pursuit, a human running behind it. Panicked, he galloped across the street. To his left, he sensed an enormous shape bearing down on him — a truck! — and lengthened his stride, shutting his eyes and expecting to feel an impact. Instead, there was a sharp screech and nothing touched him, and then he was on the other sidewalk. He heard humans yelling everywhere, and he ran another block before slowing to look behind him again. He didn't see the dog anymore. Unfortunately, though, he was out in the open on a busy street, full of cars and humans. He could hear shouts and other loud noises.

He dove into another alley and found a patch of bushes. He hid, breathing hard, all senses on alert. The dog was gone, and nothing else seemed to have followed him. He sighed, a sudden longing for the peace of the forest washing over him. From the moment he had left, he had been assaulted by strange new terrors. But he could never go back. This was his home now, and he would have to learn quickly so that he could survive. Digging into the cold, hard ground under the bush, he lay down, hoping to get some rest while he could.

He spent the next few nights exploring the city, looking for somewhere he could use as a home base. The skunk smell had weakened, but it still impacted his ability to hunt. Prey smelled him coming before he could smell them, so he was forced to eat garbage. Thankfully, in this busy part of the city, there was lots of food lying around on the streets, so he found enough to stay alive. However, he grew steadily weaker, suffering from a poor diet and a lack of deep sleep.

One night he found a small park and stopped there, sniffing around the garbage can to see what he could eat. Digging into a paper-wrapped object, he found the leftovers of a human meal. It made his lips and tongue burn as he ate it, but he didn't have too many other options. He lay down then, enjoying the brief moment of peace and quiet.

"Hey!" Scruff's eyes shot open at the sound of a gruff bark behind him. He turned his head to see a pair of coyotes staring at him, their hackles up. He jumped to his feet, lowering his head submissively.

"Get out of our territory," the female said, wrinkling her nose and turning to her partner. "I can't even breathe with him around."

"This is our park," the male added with a growl. "I don't know where you come from, but you're lucky you're just a runt or we would take this more seriously. We'll give you three seconds to get lost or we'll show you what happens to coyotes who trespass here."

Without waiting another second, Scruff turned and fled, making a mental note not to go into any more parks until he could smell better. He trotted for hours that night, feeling desperate for a quiet place he could call home. Right as the sky was beginning to lighten, the sidewalk he was following came to a *T*. In front of him was a very busy road, with train tracks running high above the road on the far side. He stopped, listening. Something was coming down the tracks, and he jumped as a sharp squeal announced the arrival of a train running overhead. He watched it in amazement as it floated over the road, running along the elevated tracks. Then, his eye was drawn to a narrow patch of green that ran under the tracks. He ran to the edge of the road, looking carefully and waiting for two cars to pass before crossing and approaching the green area. There was a tall chain-link fence that separated the sidewalk from the bushes. He trotted along it, hoping to find some way in. Up ahead, he saw some people walking toward him and changed direction, looking the other way. Finally, he saw it — a low spot dug underneath the fence. He squeezed through, diving into the deep grasses and bushes on the other side. He paused, his heart beating, trying to take stock of where he was.

He heard another elevated train coming and ducked his head, flattening his ears as it raced overhead. It was much louder from directly underneath. It passed and he waited a few more minutes, alert to any danger in the area. He got up and poked around the bushes, taking care to stay hidden from the street. He could still see the road if he peered through the fence, but now at least he had a six-foot buffer between him and it. He heard another train coming and this time it didn't scare him quite as much. Sniffing around, he overwhelmingly smelled his own skunky odour, but didn't detect any evidence of other animals. Sighing, he lay down in a small depression under a bush, hoping to be able to rest for a few moments.

Time passed and, for once, nothing made him leave his spot. He was woken every few minutes by a train going overhead, but the fence seemed to keep everything else out. With each hour that passed, he could feel his body relaxing, realizing that he finally had a place that was his. As the air cooled and the sky became dark, the roads quieted down. He stood and stretched, his stomach twisted with hunger. Now that he had a home base, he had to solve the problem of how to feed himself better.

FIFTEEN
HUMAN

Alyssa

Alyssa got the call on Monday morning at 8:15 a.m. The school principal left a panicked message on the coyote reporting line, saying that there was a "herd" of coyotes stalking the children, and although most of the animals had run off, there was still one lying there. She smiled as she listened to the message. She doubted that the coyotes had actually been stalking the kids. They had the potential to be dangerous if they were injured and cornered, but they typically didn't go out of their way to have contact with people. She frowned as she wondered about the coyote that was still there. It must be very injured or dead.

She called the school back, but the secretary couldn't get the principal on the line; she was still outside "dealing with the situation." Alyssa hung up and began to dial the number for the officers from the Ministry of the Environment, who would take away a dead or immobilized coyote. Suddenly, she paused. She hadn't been able to get an eyewitness account yet. She should probably go and check it out before assuming that the message was accurate. Who knows — maybe the coyote wasn't that injured and had figured out a way to get away. The school wasn't far from her house, anyway.

Pouring her coffee into a battered travel mug, she grabbed a coat and headed to her truck. Driving along in the dim morning light, she kept her eyes peeled for animal movement. After being a wildlife biologist in the national parks for almost a decade, she had thought that a move back to the big city would be the end of the interesting part of her career. She had been surprised to find out just how much was going on right under the noses of the millions of people who lived here. Thousands of coyotes, tens of thousands of raccoons and skunks, and all kinds of smaller mammals thrived in between the concrete towers, finding small spaces that were not covered in pavement to call their home. Right from the moment she moved here, she had been especially fascinated by the adaptability and the resourcefulness of the coyotes. It was amazing that such a large predator had learned how to live beside humans without anyone ever really becoming aware of their existence.

Pulling into the school parking lot, she saw a crowd of teachers and parents huddled in the middle of the field. The students must have been told to go inside. Well, that settled it. There must still be a coyote out there.

She walked over to the crowd, scanning the faces for someone who might be in charge. After asking a few people, she found the principal.

She stretched out her hand. "Hi, I'm Alyssa Lee. I work for the city, with Urban Wildlife Monitoring and Rescue."

"Oh, hello — thank you so much for coming out quickly. I'm Cathy Thompson, the principal here. I have to say, we just don't know what to do!" Cathy's voice was high, and she sounded on the edge of panic.

"Can you tell me what happened?"

"Well, I was inside, but Doug — he's the school custodian — ran in and told me that there were five or six coyotes on the field this morning. A whole herd of them! A parent reported it, and when he went out he saw them growling at the kids. He got a broom and went a little closer, swinging it and yelling, and they all ran away. We haven't seen them since. But there's still one there — can you see it? It's under that bush there. It hasn't moved at all." She pointed her finger at the edge of the field, where in the dark patch under a bush Alyssa could just make out the small, grey form.

"Okay, thanks. I'll check it out. Stay here and I'll let you know what I can find out." Alyssa set off toward the coyote.

"Wait — are you just going to walk up to it?" Cathy's voice was incredulous.

"I won't get too close. I'm just going to try to find out if it's alive or not." Alyssa smiled. She encountered this kind of concern every time. It must be all the big bad wolves in fairy tales that had people believing that the coyotes would surge from the ground and lock on to their throats. In fact, coyotes typically only weighed twenty to forty pounds, and human attacks were extremely rare. There had never been one in this city, and although she had heard of a few attacks in other parts of the country, she knew that they generally involved coyotes who had been fed by humans and had become habituated to the easy food source and lost their ability or drive to hunt for themselves.

When she was about five feet away, she got a better look at the coyote. It was young, only about six months or so, she figured. It looked well-fed and had soft, tawny fur covering its small body. She looked more closely, noting some open sores and scratches along its side. It must have gotten into a fight with another coyote. She wondered if the pack that had been spotted near the school had been attacking it.

"Hey, coyote!" she yelled, watching for movement. The coyote didn't stir. "You alive?" she clapped her hands a few times. Still no movement. She bent down and picked up a small stone. She threw it at the coyote, and struck it right on the cheek. Her eyes widened as the coyote let out a small yip, closer to a squeak. Its whole body shuddered, and it began to get up, a high yelp of pain escaping as it struggled onto three legs. It was hard to watch. Its eyes blinked, and it shook its head. It held its front right paw up off the ground — it must be seriously injured. Then, after only a few seconds of standing, it fell back into the dirt. It mewed softly a few times, almost like a cat, and then was still again.

Alyssa nodded and turned to walk quickly back to the principal. "It's still alive, but it isn't mobile. I think it's a leg issue, and maybe some infection, too. It's so young that it actually might have a chance — I'll get a volunteer from our organization and we'll take it back to our rehabilitation centre. It's a long shot, but we'll see what we can do."

A man, probably a parent, was standing nearby and overheard them. He stepped in with a frown. "You are going to try to heal it? Why don't you just … take care of it?"

"Well, we do put down animals, yes. But we try to heal them if it's an injury that we think we can help with. Sometimes it works."

"I don't know. I think you should just kill it. It's obviously a danger." The man shook his head. Alyssa sighed, not wanting to get into a long and drawn-out conversation, and turned her body slightly so she was facing Cathy more directly. "Cathy, I need you to keep everyone away from the coyote. And someone needs to keep an eye on it, in case it tries to go somewhere. It won't get far, in any case. I should be back in less than an hour."

Cathy nodded. "Okay. I'll get the custodian to stay out here until you get back." She beckoned a tall, older man over and began to explain the situation to him. Alyssa nodded and headed back to her car, and began calling volunteers.

In just over an hour, Alyssa had rounded up a long-time volunteer, James, and collected her supplies from the office. She had with her a metal rod with a Y-prong at the end, two nets that looked a bit like oversized butterfly nets, and a large kennel. James met her at the parking lot with an excited smile. Their volunteers spent most of the time in the office talking to people on the phone about coyote sightings and questions. Getting an opportunity to rescue a coyote was a fairly rare occurrence. In the last year, they had captured only four coyotes. Two of them had been too sick and had died, but two of them had been rehabilitated and released.

"Can you help me carry this stuff over?" she asked. Together, they carried the kennel to within seven feet of the coyote. It didn't stir. Then, working carefully, she positioned the Y-prong onto the pup's neck. It woke up and began to struggle, panic giving it a rush of energy. However, with its neck pinned to the ground, it couldn't get up at all. James put the net over it, and then brought the kennel closer. Carefully steering its direction with the rod, Alyssa guided the panicked coyote into the crate. James pushed the door shut and latched it. There were a few weak howls, and then silence. They both took a big breath, and smiled at one another.

"Nice work," she said.

"That was great!" he exclaimed as he gave her a high-five. She grinned at his enthusiasm.

"Well, we'll have to bring it in and take a closer look. It's in pretty rough shape right now."

James nodded, and together they carried the crate to the back of her car. The coyote made a sad crying sound from inside, and she could smell that it had defecated into the crate. This was typical; the animal was terrified. Once it was in the back of her truck, she told James to pop by later that day to find out how it was doing, and she headed for the rehabilitation centre.

SIXTEEN
INSIDE

Pica

Terror gripped her. Pica was trapped in a small box and there was a loud rumbling and shaking from all around her. The ground moved underneath her unexpectedly, causing her body to roll from one side of the box to the other. A few times she tried to stand and look outside, but she was so unsteady that whenever the ground shifted she fell back down again.

After what seemed like a long period of time, the noise and the shaking stopped. She heard rocks crunching and a loud screech, and then light filtered into the box, blinding her after the darkness. She saw the shadow of a human and heard talking. Yelping weakly, she shoved herself to the far end of the box, trying to get away. It was impossible. She could smell humans surrounding the box, their odd chemical smells filling her nostrils and blocking out everything else. Her box was carried inside a building and then everything was quiet.

Pica opened her eyes cautiously and peeked out of the bars of the box. She saw a pair of dark human eyes staring back at her. Pica inhaled with fear — direct eye contact at such close range set off all of her alarm bells. She braced herself for an attack. The minutes passed, and the woman did not move. Pica's breathing slowed. Then her breathing quickened again as the woman stretched her hand out. Pica let out a weak, low growl as the woman touched the box. Pica heard a squeaking sound, and the front of the box popped open. The woman moved away then, taking a few steps backwards.

Pica slowly pulled herself out from the box, standing shakily in the new space. Tall concrete walls stretched up on all sides and overhead. There were a few objects in the room, and some small windows through which she could see trees. The ground under her feet was hard and her nails felt funny pressed against it. There was the smell of many other animals in the room, and also the smell of fear.

She looked around weakly, and saw a bowl of water beside her. She was suddenly aware of a massive thirst. Keeping one eye on the woman, she sniffed the water. It smelled good, but the container that it was in smelled like other animals. She didn't quite trust it. Eventually, though, her thirst overcame her, and she dropped her head to drink. Immediately, something dark passed over her eyes and she felt the woman's hands on her head. Thick straps surrounded her jaws, pressing them together, and she couldn't drink anymore. She turned her head and tried to bite the woman, but her mouth wouldn't open. She yelped in fear, but even her yelp sounded funny. She felt something burn into her back hip, and continued to struggle for a few more seconds. Slowly, then, she felt her desire to resist melt away, and began to feel very calm.

She ceased to care as the woman picked her up off the ground, carrying her to a basin on the other side of the room. When her whole body was dipped into a wet, stinging liquid, she did gasp and jerk her head, but even then, the fear and resistance slipped away. She could feel the liquid burning into her cuts, but her eyelids dipped closed and the experiences melted around her, slipping away whenever she tried to grasp them.

Over the next hour, she was vaguely aware of being carried to some other places, picked up and put down, poked and prodded, but finally she was returned to the box and she fell into a deep sleep. When she woke, she was groggy. She was still in the box, but smelled grass and plants around her, and knew she wasn't in the concrete room anymore. All around her was light and fresh air. She raised her head, shaking her ears to clear them. The straps were no longer on her jaw, but something was stuck around her neck, making it so that she couldn't see or scratch her body. Also, there was something very firm wrapped around her bad leg. She struggled to get the objects off, but it was impossible.

Peering out of the box, Pica saw she was in the corner of a very small grassy area surrounded by a high chain-link fence. Through the fence she could see trees, and she could also smell water and hear a busy road nearby. She couldn't see or smell any humans. She put her leg down on the ground and was surprised that the pain seemed less sharp than it had before. Suddenly, she was distracted by the smell of something delicious. She saw a bowl with food in it at the other end of her box. It was fresh meat. Dipping her head down, the object around her neck banging against the ground, she managed to get her head low enough to get some food. It was delicious.

Suddenly, she tensed. Something didn't seem right. This was too easy. She swallowed the bite and then, with a regretful look, backed away, curling up in the far end of the box. She spent a few more minutes trying to get the thing off her neck, and when she couldn't budge it, lay down with a sigh. She was stuck for now, and still so sleepy. She curled up and fell asleep again.

When she woke up again, it was dark. Nothing had changed. She didn't smell humans anymore, but the smell of the meat was now overpowering, and she realized how hungry she was. She hobbled over and finished it, no longer caring if it was a trap. She drank deeply from the water beside her food. Her belly full, she now became more aware of her leg throbbing. She whined for a few minutes, wondering where she was and what was going to happen to her. She gradually began to feel sleepy again, and curling up in the corner seemed like a relief.

Alyssa

Driving home that night, Alyssa couldn't stop thinking about the little female coyote. Callie — she knew she wasn't supposed to give it a name, but it had just popped into her head and now she couldn't help it — was a tough little fighter. After giving her a full checkup today, she had found evidence of a severe eye infection that had probably made her mostly blind in one eye, some infected wounds, and an injured leg. Given the amount of time that had passed since the injuries were inflicted, it was a wonder the little thing was alive at all.

Luckily, they had a vet who worked regularly with their organization, and he had dropped by to help as much as he could. Alyssa had given Callie a disinfecting bath for her wounds, and the vet had splinted and bandaged the leg. There was nothing she could do about the eye, but she had seen other coyotes with eye issues, and they were sometimes able to survive. She felt pretty confident that they would be able to heal the infection on the coyote's body, but given the extent of her leg injury, Alyssa figured that Callie had about a 50 percent chance of healing well enough to be released. The next few days would be crucial — if Callie would eat and rest, it would give her body the chance to begin repairing itself.

The next day, Alyssa drove into work early and walked softly over to the enclosure, unsure of what she would find. As she approached, she saw Callie's head pop up and glare at her through the bars of the crate. She gave a low growl. Alyssa sighed with relief. She had made it through the night and was on her feet — that was a good sign. A few hours later, she put some more food out for her. This was the only time when Callie would see food coming from a human, because there was really no other way as long as she was still in the crate. Soon, though, they would let her out into the enclosure, and try to deliver the food when she was asleep. This would prevent her from becoming too habituated to the idea of food coming directly from people.

Habituation to humans, especially seeing them as the best food source, was the most dangerous part of rehabilitation. If a coyote lost its fear of humans, they would inevitably get another call a week after release to tell them that it was following people around, waiting for some more food. Then the coyote would have to be put down. Distrust of humans was what kept coyotes alive in the city.

Despite the fact that coyote attacks were exceedingly rare, people were still very nervous about seeing them out in the open during the daytime. If only they knew how many coyotes were under their noses at all times, carefully concealed in the shadows of the bushes, they would be shocked. In their city alone, estimates of the number of coyotes ranged from four hundred to six hundred, and a few thousand more in the suburbs surrounding the city. It was amazing that the coyotes, given their numbers, managed to stay so out of sight.

Alyssa didn't bother Callie that day, allowing her the time and space to heal. However, the next day she put a muzzle on her again and took her in for another antibiotic bath. Seeing the still-angry wounds on her side and back, she frowned, doubts resurfacing about Callie's ability to survive. The wounds were still red and irritated, although they didn't look worse than two days ago, which was one good thing. Looking at all of the injuries together, it was clear that the little coyote had had a tough go of it. Alyssa shook her head as she gently bathed the pup, wondering what kind of troubles Callie had gotten into in her life so far. She looked down at the sweet, furry face, and as she smiled, she reminded herself not to get too attached. She checked the bandages on the leg, and then put Callie back in the crate, where she cowered in the corner, glaring at Alyssa.

It was another week before the vet decided that Callie could move from the crate into the small grass enclosure, beginning to put some weight onto her leg. Alyssa was glad — she could now stop working so closely with the coyote, and feeding could become a bit more natural. She also felt a little bit sad — she wished that she could have the time to gain the small coyote's trust. But she was well aware that this would endanger Callie later, because it was necessary for her to remain wary of people. So Alyssa watched Callie hop around from the safety of the video camera mounted on the fence of the enclosure. She shook her head. Despite the fact that the little pup was doing better, she still wasn't confident that Callie would be able to make it.

SEVENTEEN
MALA

Scruff

Because there was no other option, Scruff established his new home base under the elevated train. The weeks passed in a hungry blur as he attempted to survive on his own. At night he roamed the back alleys, looking for rodents and garbage. He found some edible plants and grass in a few of the green patches outside a building. He tried to stay away from other coyotes and humans, but it was difficult. The streets were so busy here that he had a smaller window of time at night in which to roam and hunt. All the parks and the quieter streets were well defended by other coyotes, and he had to steer clear of them. Each morning, he returned to his patch of weeds under the train, hungry and disheartened.

However, with each day, he learned something new that helped him to survive. He distracted himself from his sadness by figuring out new ways to get food, sneaking through back alleys and finding all of the spots where the garbage wasn't well protected. The change in diet from mostly natural to more garbage wreaked havoc on his digestive system, but he had no choice, eating whatever he could find.

However, even as he gained more survival skills, the weather got worse. The days grew shorter and colder. One night, he was skulking behind a restaurant, looking for rats that liked to congregate around the garbage bins, when he felt an odd wetness hit his nose. It burned, and then felt very cold and damp. He looked up to see where it was coming from, and more cold-hot pieces hit his eyes. Blinking, he saw that there were pieces of white fluff falling from the sky everywhere. It was similar to rain but much colder. He jumped under a small awning and watched it fall slowly down, sticking for a moment on the ground before melting away. He smiled. It was odd and beautiful.

The beauty was fleeting. As the night wore on, the stuff began to stick to the ground. It was cold on his paws, and the wind made his wet fur freeze. Shivering, he trotted back early to his home base before the night had ended. He found a spot under the bushes where the snow could not penetrate and curled up in a tight ball, tucking his nose under his fur. Out of the wind and on top of the dirt, he felt a little warmer, but knew that this might be a new and very serious threat.

In the days after the first snow, Scruff was exhausted. He wasn't able to sleep well, curled up and shivering against the frozen ground. He found it more tiring to travel in the soft, mushy, white stuff, and he didn't find much food. On the third night, as his stomach felt particularly empty, he set off with grim determination. He would find food no matter what. He had to.

He headed along his usual route, following a back alley behind a busy street. Wind funnelled into the alley, blowing ice into his fur. The cold bit into his exposed skin and he shivered. He turned around, keeping his back to the wind, and decided to try a new route. Maybe it would be less windy somewhere else.

A few blocks in the other direction, he came across a parking lot he had never seen before. He smelled that it was another coyote's territory, and was about to keep moving when he saw a human dumping something that smelled delicious into a large metal container. He strained forward, sniffing delicately. It was meat — he was sure of it — and something sweet, too. His eyes widened as he saw some of the items from the boxes miss the side of the bin and tumble onto the pavement. The human either didn't mind or didn't notice, returning quickly to the building. Scruff crept closer, sniffing carefully. His stomach rumbled and he decided to chance it.

Reaching the side of the container, he detected a strong rodent scent, mixed with the meaty garbage smell. Ears perked, he homed in on the little rustles of the rats who were eating near the Dumpster. Rounding the side, he saw one and fluidly leapt toward it. With two graceful bounds he was on it, taking it completely by surprise and killing it instantly. He ate the whole thing hungrily and then began eating the human food. Just as he was crunching on a vegetable, he caught a faint smell — another coyote. He stopped short, sniffing the air with each nostril — it was the coyotes who lived here! He had to get away immediately. Pivoting, he took off at a gallop back to the alley. As he glanced behind him, he saw two large silhouettes pursuing him.

Feeling the rush of adrenaline, he increased his pace, leaning his head forward to lengthen his stride, turning left out of the alley and onto the street. The street sloped sharply downhill toward a big highway. He ran halfway there and flicked his ears back to see if he was still being pursued. He chanced a glance behind him, and his eyes widened when he saw the two coyotes barrelling toward him, their sounds muffled by the increasing level of noise on the highway. They must be chasing him to the edge of their territory. The only problem was that he didn't know where that edge was. He dashed down the hill without a plan, stopping at the grass that marked the edge of the on-ramp to the highway. He looked in front of him at the almost constant stream of cars. Their tires made high-pitched hissing noises on the wet road. He looked behind him again. The two coyotes were almost on him now.

"We'll teach you to stay out of our territory!" the female barked at him, baring her teeth. She was tall and lean, her grey eyes flashing with anger. Recoiling, Scruff found himself running along the edge of the highway. He thought desperately that if he crossed it, they probably wouldn't follow. It might be his only chance. Seeing a small gap in the oncoming traffic, he leapt into the road and began to run across. The wind swirled hard from all directions, and lights blinded him. He raced for the other side, not seeing anything anymore. He felt a particularly strong wind behind him and heard horns blaring and the screeching of tires on pavement. He felt dirt under his paws again and tumbled down an embankment — he was across!

He looked back, shuddering, but didn't see the coyotes. He felt his heart beating twice as fast as usual, and he couldn't think. He ran a little farther away and then paused, trying to collect himself. He didn't want to try crossing the road again, but he didn't know how else to get back to his home. He decided to follow the road downhill to see if there would be a better place to cross.

The rain let up as he trotted along, and a few stars poked out. He didn't feel cold, still filled with adrenaline. He travelled for about twenty minutes, following the slope downhill, keeping the highway within earshot to his left. It became clear to him that finding a safe spot to cross was going to be very difficult.

Just then, he was distracted by a salty odour that was very new to him — was it a kind of food? A new kind of territory? As he continued, it got stronger, but all the houses to his right blocked his view of what it might be. Eventually, his curiosity won out and he left the highway behind, trotting down steep embankments now, threading his way through backyards and alleys. As the smell increased, he became aware of a sound — a rhythmic splashing. Then, suddenly, he was there.

The snow disappeared at the edge of a vast expanse of water. He stepped out onto grey earth, and it felt nothing like dirt. It moved underneath him, destabilizing him. It was both soft and scratchy. Scattered around were large logs and slimy, green pieces of something that smelled salty. The grey earth led to the edge of the dark grey water, water so much larger than the pond at the golf course that he didn't know what to call it. He decided to call it the Giant Pond. A loud shushing noise filled his ears.

He approached the water cautiously, but suddenly it was chasing him, soaking his legs with icy water. He barked at it angrily. He watched it for a minute, and then realized how thirsty he was. He ran toward it, trying to lap at it before it came back at him. Immediately he spat it out. It was salty and weird tasting. He barked at it again.

Behind him, he heard a laugh. He froze, turning to see a very old female coyote perched at the top of the embankment, watching him. Her grey fur was patchy, but he could see strongly defined muscles underneath. She barked a friendly greeting. He backed away slowly, looking around for his escape options just in case.

"Hey — don't run away!" she yelled at him over the whooshing of the water, coming toward him. "Who are you? I've never seen you around here before."

"I'm not from here. I'm just passing through." He found himself backing up a little more, trying to keep some distance from her, but then the water lapped his legs from behind and he jumped toward her, yelping.

"Looks like you've never seen the ocean before!" she laughed.

"The ocean?" He decided not to mention to her about the Giant Pond.

"Anyway, what brings you here, ah — what's your name?"

"Scruff." After that word, Scruff found himself hesitating. He wasn't sure what to say. The truth seemed very long and complex.

The old coyote looked at him with curiosity, seemingly unfazed by his lack of explanation. "You don't have to act like I'm about to eat you. I've got better things to do than terrorize scrawny little coyotes. I'm just curious — I don't see young pups on their own very often around here. Where's your family?"

"I don't have a family."

"Well, okay, then. Everyone's story is different." She didn't push him for more, pausing before continuing. "Well, Scruff, nice to meet you. I'm Mala."

Scruff took a breath, finally relaxing. This was the first coyote he'd met since leaving the hillside who didn't greet him with aggression. In fact, it had been a while since he'd had a conversation with anyone.

"Is this your territory?" he blurted out, curious.

Mala threw back her head, laughing. "Who would live here on this smelly beach? No, I have a good territory not far from here, with my family. I just pass through here looking for food. It's not a great spot, but sometimes I find rats around. Gotta clear out before day, though. Lots of humans come through here."

"Oh." Scruff was a little disappointed. He knew that daylight would be coming in just a few hours and felt exhausted at the thought of leaving to find somewhere to spend the day.

"I guess you'll be looking for somewhere to go, huh?" she asked, seeming to read his mind.

Scruff hesitated, then decided to open up a little bit. "I crossed the highway to get away from some coyotes, and I don't really want to try that again. I need to find somewhere to cross back."

Mala barked out a laugh. "You crossed that highway? What are you, crazy? I'm shocked you didn't get flattened!" She paused, thinking. "You know, the only way I know to get back across is pretty difficult. If you follow the shoreline — the side of the ocean — for a whole night, you'll reach a park. It's a really huge park — beautiful. The highway lifts up off the ground there and goes over the ocean to the other side. It's called a bridge, and it connects this land with the land on the other side of the water." She pointed with her nose to the twinkling lights shining from across the water. "There, right where the bridge lifts up, you can just walk right underneath it, and then exit the park on the other side. And there you go, you'll be on the other side of the highway."

Scruff felt his heart lifting. "Thanks, that doesn't sound too hard."

"Well, the problem is that Storm and her pack control the park. They're strong and they don't let coyotes pass through. They'll kill to protect their territory, because it's the best around."

The word *kill* bounced around Scruff's mind, bringing up images of blood and gnashing teeth, and a body falling through the darkness. He shivered, feeling shame deep inside of him. It took him a moment to tune back into what Mala was saying.

"— possible, if you were desperate. But it is pretty risky. You'd have to cross during the middle of the day. That way Storm and her pack might be asleep. Of course, the humans will see you, but I think they are less dangerous than the alternative."

"How do you know all of this?"

"Well, I actually came from the lands on the other side of the water, many years ago." Mala nodded her head at the little twinkling lights across the ocean.

"From all the way over there? On the far side of the bridge?"

She smiled. "Yes, hard to believe, right? It seems so long ago now. Those lights are at the edge of the Wild Lands. It was spring, many years ago, and I was ready to move on from my parents. I felt restless, so one night I followed the path on the side of the bridge. I was scared, but I was too proud to turn around, so I ducked through the park and arrived here. It was possible back then because Storm and her pack-mates weren't defending the park yet. Anyway, I ended up meeting my mate, and then we had pups, so I never went back."

"What was it like there, on the other side? In the Wild Lands?"

"Well," Mala sighed. "It's different. There are fewer humans, many more green spaces. It can be harder to find food, which is odd, because there is more space in general. I'm pretty used to the way it is over here, and my memory isn't so good anymore. But from what I remember, it's beautiful." She paused, and then looked at him with a smile. "Anyway, I should go. I need to find some mice before it gets light."

"Thanks for all of the information." Scruff stood there, reluctant to leave the first friendly face he had met in months. Mala gave him a last quick smile and scrambled back up the embankment, disappearing into a yard. Scruff felt an intense loneliness, wanting to follow her. Knowing that she couldn't help him, he sighed and began to plan his next moves. If what she said was true, he only had an hour or two before this beach would be no longer safe. He followed her advice and headed along the shoreline, the immense darkness of the sky and ocean wrapping around him.

EIGHTEEN
LOST

Pica

Many days passed in the enclosure. Pica began to feel a little bit better each day, and soon the most painful aspect was boredom. The only thing that broke the monotony was waking up and looking around for food. She found herself constantly wondering about what had happened to her family. Where were they? Had they found a safe home? What had they thought when they came back to the field for her and discovered that she was gone? That last thought was the most hurtful of all. They surely thought she was dead now, and there was nothing she could do about it. Her heart ached thinking of how they wouldn't even be looking for her anymore. Even if she did manage to escape, how would she ever find them again?

One day dawned like any other. Pica was sleeping soundly in her small den, a crate set in the corner of the enclosure. The crate was small and dark, and gave her a sense of security when she slept. This morning, though, she was woken by a loud clanging noise. Jumping up, she discovered that a door now blocked the entrance to the crate — she was locked in! She heard new human voices, and then the ground was shaking. Suddenly, she realized the crate was moving.

There were bursts of new sights and smells but she couldn't make sense of them through her panic. Very soon, though, the den stopped moving and the door opened again. Pica stood still for a few moments, afraid to move, and then took a step forward to peer out. She was in a new enclosure. This one was bigger than the last, and had some clumps of bushes in it. She ran across to the bushes as fast as her stiff leg would allow her, and squeezed underneath them.

In this new place, the sound of traffic was a little bit louder, but she heard humans less often. At first, she was hopeful that she would be able to find a way to escape, because there were so many more possibilities than in the last enclosure. However, after systematically investigating every single corner of the pen, she could not find a single weakness. After a few long and tiring hours of trying, she concluded that it would be impossible to chew or dig her way out.

As the days passed, boredom found her again. When she was lying down, she missed the warm fur of her mother curled up tightly around her. When the snow first fell, she puzzled over it, wishing she could experience it with her siblings. It was no fun to play in it alone. Every time she saw something new, she felt sad because there was no one to share it with.

Then, one day, the woman returned. Using a long stick, she managed to pin Pica's head to the ground. Pica struggled and cried out, trying her best to get away, but she was helpless. She couldn't believe it was happening again. The woman slipped the straps over Pica's mouth and put her in the crate. The next hour was traumatizing, as the woman and another human pushed and prodded at her. When they were done, she was brought to a place she had never been before. She was breathing hard as the woman took off the straps and released her, and she ran to the far corner as fast as she could, cowering behind a tree.

The woman left, and a few minutes later, Pica's heart slowed. When she could think clearly, she realized with surprise that she no longer had anything on her leg or her neck. She was free of all the odd contraptions that the humans had put on her. Next, she realized that she was standing almost naturally on all four legs! Her bad leg felt tender but the sharp pain from before was gone. She looked around her new space with wonder. There were trees, bushes, and a small pond. It was much bigger than the previous enclosures. She spent the next hour gingerly walking around, sniffing every inch of it. She smelled other coyotes, squirrels, and birds, but there didn't seem to be any animals there at the moment.

When she had satisfied her curiosity, she sat down and, now free of the object around her neck, inspected her sides and stomach. Licking carefully at first, she was surprised to notice that her wounds didn't feel sore anymore. She could feel the rough lines of scarring, but overall, she felt pretty good. Feeling an odd wave of euphoria wash over her, she jumped up, spinning around and running as fast as she could toward the other end of the pen. She felt an ache in her leg, but it wasn't terrible. When she got to the edge, she leaned to the side, cornering to turn in the other direction. After a few seconds like this, her brain felt calmer and she stopped, breathing hard. It had been so long since she had run.

The euphoria wore off quickly, and the day passed like any other. She walked around, waiting for something to happen, but the day passed without event and it became night. She tucked herself under some bushes with a sigh. She was surprised at how quickly her earlier joy had worn off. Life here had tended to alternate between traumatizing and boring, and she had no control over when anything happened. She was lonely and wondered how long she would be here. Would she die here? With that thought, she laid her head down and fell asleep.

More days passed like this, and Pica began to lose all hope. However, one day, something important changed. There was a small door in the fencing of the enclosure, and today it opened for the first time with a squeak. She turned her head listlessly, but her eyes opened wide as she glimpsed a streak of soft brown fur. She yelped, jumping up and backwards. What was it? A live rabbit shot through the door and into the enclosure. Her heart started pounding, and instinctively, she froze. The rabbit, now in the middle of the enclosure, froze as well. For a moment, they stared at one another. Pica held her breath. This was by far the most interesting thing that had happened to her since she arrived.

It only took Pica about five seconds to corner and kill the animal. She noticed that it was slower than the rabbits she had seen before, and although she wondered briefly why that was, the thrill of catching and eating her prey overtook any other thought. Something in her body woke up, and for the rest of the day, she couldn't stop trotting around the enclosure, smiling to herself and again sniffing the trail that the rabbit had taken when trying to evade her. She replayed the chase in her mind, savouring the moment where she had pounced and felt the rabbit beneath her paws. It had been so easy! Even though her leg still felt a little stiff and weak, the chase had felt fluid and natural. She couldn't lie down, pacing around and wondering if it would happen again.

And it did. Day after day, live prey was pushed into the enclosure for her to eat. Each animal seemed to be more agile than the last, challenging her to practise her intense focus, following their flight closely, cutting from side to side and pouncing at the right time. She didn't always get them the first time, and was often slightly off her mark on the pounce, but with every success she became more confident. She had never before had such a frequent opportunity to practise her pouncing, and felt happy knowing she was getting better.

Days passed and her leg began to feel almost normal again. She noticed her fur growing back thickly, and her back and side didn't feel sore anymore when she cleaned herself. She still felt lonely, but at least she finally had something to look forward to each day.

Alyssa

Alyssa arrived at work that day feeling oddly emotional. After many weeks of treating little Callie, they had decided that she was ready for release. It had been a long journey, but she looked fit and healthy, with only a few patchy areas on her fur indicating that anything had been wrong. Her eye had not improved, and they were fairly certain she was completely blind on that side. Despite this, she had shown herself able to catch her own prey, so there was no reason to keep her anymore.

Although she was happy to see Callie get another chance, Alyssa worried. It was still the middle of winter, and cold. Callie was still so young, probably only eight or nine months old, and if she didn't reunite with her pack again, she would find it very hard to fend for herself. She might unwittingly enter a rival pack's territory, or have forgotten how to navigate streets and traffic. Alyssa wanted to know what would happen to Callie, but knew that after releasing her back into the city, she would probably never see the little coyote again.

They had debated for a long time about where to release Callie. Generally, they tried to release the animals in the spot where they had been captured. If they did this, the animal would have its bearings and be much more likely to find its family again. She had heard of stories where people released an animal somewhere new, and inevitably it would be a disaster, the animal either getting killed by rival coyotes or travelling great distances trying to find its way back home. However, the schoolyard was less than ideal as a release point. After being given her freedom, Callie would have to figure out somewhere else to go by the time the kids arrived at school. After much back and forth, the decision was finally made. They would release her on Friday night in the schoolyard so she would have a whole weekend to find her pack or a new home.

Alyssa waited until it got dark, grabbed a mug of tea, and found the volunteer, Sarah, who would be helping her. They loaded Callie's crate into the back of her truck and drove to the schoolyard. Sarah tried to make conversation in the passenger seat, but Alyssa didn't feel like chatting, and gave mostly one-syllable responses. Finally, they were there. They carefully put the crate down, opened the door, and returned to the truck, climbing in the cab to watch. A few seconds later, they saw a slim, grey shadow slip out from the crate, gallop across the field, and disappear into the bushes at the far end. Alyssa watched, feeling sad to see her go, but also joyful that they had been able to give her a chance. They loaded the crate back into the truck, and without a word, Alyssa turned on the engine and drove away. Now, she could only hope that she never heard about this little coyote again.

Pica

The field was dark and a cold, icy layer covered the grass. Pica shivered. She did a slow lap of the field, sniffing every tree and bush. She could hardly believe that she was free. At first she was exuberant — she knew where she was! Soon, though, she realized with a sinking heart that there wasn't a single trace of her family in the area. They were long gone. She spent the evening moving in ever-increasing circles, desperate to find their scent. However, after many long hours of searching, she was left with aching paws, a sore back leg, and a sense of hopelessness. It had been weeks, maybe months, since her pack had been here. By now, they could be anywhere.

She found herself shivering as the sky slowly began to lighten. It took a bit of searching to find a quiet spot in a back alley where she could settle down, out of sight. It wasn't a great spot, but it would have to do for the day. She needed time to make a plan. All day she lay restlessly, thinking about her options. She could strike out in a random direction each night, hoping her family had not gone too far and that she would eventually pick up on a scent trail. She could look for a new home base, and then try to explore from there. Or maybe if she just picked a direction, she would get lucky. The hopeless feeling began to well up in her. There were endless places where her family could be, and exploring the city to look for them was difficult and dangerous. She still wasn't that confident in finding food, crossing streets, and avoiding other coyotes. How was she going to survive at all, let alone survive while looking for them?

Night finally fell, and Pica got up and stretched. Her leg was stiff, but not sore. She hadn't come to any decisions and decided to just head in any direction until she thought of a better plan. She could look for food along the way. She cautiously left her sleeping spot and walked along the alley, keeping her nose and ears alert for signs of danger or food. The night was cold and clear and a small sliver of moon gave her some light to see by. She tried to remember all of the instructions her parents had given her for travelling through the city. Slowly, she made her way forward, ducking often to hide from cars, and using her nose to search for food.

Pica changed direction frequently, avoiding any scent markings that indicated other coyote territory. Other than a few skunks and raccoons, she didn't see any animals. Then, cutting through the cold night air, she heard a familiar sound. A high blast followed by a deep, low rumbling. A train! Memories of her journey fleeing the hillside rushed back at her. Drawn to the familiar memories, she found herself heading toward the sound, and a few minutes later, she reached a knoll that looked down onto the train track. She recognized the smells and knew that she had passed through here before with her family.

An odd feeling shivered through her body. Standing on the ties, she felt closer than ever to her family. From here, she knew where she was and how to get back to the hillside. Even though she knew that her family was no longer living there, she longed to feel like she was in a familiar place again. Then, she had a thought. There were lots of coyotes in the area around the hillside that had known her parents. They weren't all as aggressive as Jagger. Maybe, if she returned to the area, she could ask them if they had heard anything about her family. It was a long shot, but one of them might know something.

An image of Jagger's sneering face flashed through her mind. If he caught her in the area, she had no doubt that he would try to kill her. However, if she didn't find out more information, she had no hope of finding her family, and that prospect was worse than potentially meeting Jagger. Taking a deep breath, she made the decision to turn left on the train tracks, and return to her childhood home.

NINETEEN
DECISION

Scruff

After leaving Mala behind, Scruff continued on until he arrived at a small rocky beach next to the ocean. There, a storm drain poured dirty water onto the sand, and it trickled out to the ocean, smelling like gasoline and metal. Bits of plastic and metal littered the beach. Other than the smell, it was a pretty good spot. Lots of bushes, no other coyote smell, and there was less snow here, right by the water. He curled up on a soft patch of green ground, tucked under a fat cedar bush, and fell asleep.

He woke a few hours later, feeling rested. As he stood, his paws throbbed a bit, and as he stretched, he could feel his hind leg muscles. The strain of the last few days was taking its toll. He was also extremely hungry and thirsty.

He hesitated, thinking about his next move. He knew he couldn't make his home here, and thought more about what Mala had said about the land on the other side of the bridge. Maybe if he went there he would get away from the feelings of guilt and sadness that had followed him ever since leaving the hillside.

He trotted down to the water, sniffing and looking around. By the muted traffic sounds and the light, it appeared to be around the middle of the day. He decided to continue travelling, and if he reached the park before dusk, he would try to cross. He would give himself the day to think about whether he wanted to try going over the bridge or whether he would return to his train spot.

His progress was much slower than he had expected. The beach didn't run continuously along next to the water, but was interrupted often by buildings, people, parking lots, and piers. Because it was the middle of the day, it was difficult to find alleys and backyards quiet enough to allow him to continue travelling without being spotted.

Finally, coming around the corner of a quiet stretch of beach, he smelled it. The familiar scent of pine and cedar trees, and fresh, clean air blowing toward him. It was intoxicating, the new smells sweetly humming on top of the rest of the strong, oily city odours. He spotted a long stretch of forest alongside the water, just a short walk away. He paused and looked out over the ocean. He wanted so much to push on, but had to accept that the light was quickly fading. He felt strong, but not strong enough to enter a dangerous territory at dusk, when Storm and her pack would likely be active.

He would find a spot to wait out the night, and then he would attempt the crossing the next day.

He found a quiet cluster of bushes beside a parking lot and, after investigating the area, decided it would be safe for the night. He closed his eyes, but thoughts kept crowding his brain. Lamar falling into the hole. Pica's large, sad eyes. Jagger's face, cold and expressionless. His mother's gentle tongue. All of the sadness of his life seemed to crowd in to find somewhere in his brain to sit, making him feel heavier and heavier. A vision of Lamar, standing strong with hackles raised, pushed in front of all his other thoughts. He sighed, frustrated, and stood, making three more circles in the dirt before curling up again. He tried to push the thoughts from his mind. But they stayed, weighing on him.

He wondered whether it would be possible to leave them behind simply by crossing the bridge. Behind tightly closed eyes, Lamar appeared again, and then Jagger, too. They were both staring at him. Suddenly, an old thought resurfaced, making him open his eyes in surprise. Had Jagger been telling him the truth about his family? Did Lamar really kill his parents? He had tried not to think about this for a long time, but now that it had come up, he couldn't stop. Jagger had been so good to him when he was a pup — he wouldn't be alive without him. However, Jagger had lied about his plans to kill Lamar. How could he be sure that Jagger had told the truth about the deaths of Scruff's parents?

His mind raced. If Lamar hadn't killed his parents, who had? Was Jagger guilty? But if so, why would he have rescued Scruff? He closed his eyes again, trying to block out all of the unsettling questions. There was nothing he could do about it right now.

Many hours later, he finally sensed dawn. Standing up, he felt heavy. It was still quite early, but he decided to get going. He could find some more food before getting to the forest, and wait at the edge until it was the right time. He couldn't stay still anymore, trapped with his thoughts.

An hour later he found himself at the end of an alley that opened out to the park. He stopped behind a garbage bin to observe the situation. In front of him was a soft, sandy beach. There were a few humans walking and jogging along it, but it was still early morning and it was mostly quiet. On his left was the ocean, and to the right of the beach was a busy road that ran alongside the ocean as far as he could see.

He found a bush to hide under and surveyed the scene, waiting patiently as the sun rose higher in the sky. He wanted to make sure that Storm and her pack had the highest chance of being asleep. The beach became busier, with some people riding bikes, walking their dogs, and sitting on benches. It seemed now like it was almost swarming with humans, and he had no idea how he was going to get through them all. He had never willingly launched himself into the open in an area full of humans in the broad daylight.

Finally, he couldn't delay any longer. The sun was directly above him. With a deep breath, he eased out from under the bush and trotted into the open. He had his eye on a clump of bushes at the far end of the beach — if he could just get through the crowds, it looked like a safe sanctuary.

Almost immediately, a bike loomed in front of him, and he heard screeching brakes and shouting. He shut his eyes and dove to the side, waiting to feel the impact. He felt only the sidewalk. Getting up, he saw the bike had stopped just a few feet from where he stood, and he took off away from it at a full gallop. Humans scattered to the side of the path as he ran along it. He chose the straightest route to the bushes and tried to get there as quickly as he could. The beach was longer than he had expected.

He was breathing hard now. Sustaining a gallop for more than a minute was something he rarely did. Finally, he reached the bushes, which marked the edge of the forest. This made him nervous, because he didn't know where Storm and her pack would be hanging out. His only option, if he wanted to avoid the forest, was to follow a narrow pathway clogged by humans that bordered the water. He took a few deep breaths, and then set off again into the crowds, shivering as his fur made gentle contact with one of the humans. He heard shouts from all sides, and braced himself, but nothing hit him.

A few minutes later, something above him caught his eye. He looked up and saw a massive metal bridge reaching out over the water as far as he could see. This must be the bridge to the new land! The sound of cars and trucks driving on it was deafening. There was an open area directly under the bridge, with low scrubby bushes and no humans, and he stopped there to catch his breath. On both sides of him now was water. The park was essentially a small peninsula, and he had reached the tip.

He sat there, the noise over his head making it hard to think. Was he really ready to leave this world behind and try out a new life on the other side of the bridge? He was so close to just getting up and doing it, but something held him back. His thoughts returned to his parents. Could he really go on without ever knowing the truth about his family? Scruff felt his head pounding. He had so many unanswered questions.

Then, all of a sudden, it was clear to him. He had to go back to the hillside and confront Jagger, make him tell the truth. He needed to know what had happened to his family and why he had grown up with Jagger. He didn't know what he would do with the information, but he knew instinctively that without it, he wouldn't be able to start fresh.

Without any further thought or planning, he rejoined the human path. The humans continued to react with shouts and screaming, but he began to gain confidence as nothing attacked him. He found himself wondering what kind of secret danger they posed. Even though they were close, they didn't do anything to hurt him. This was definitely better than dealing with Storm.

Suddenly, Scruff felt something sting the back of his head. He looked back, and saw some humans throwing rocks and sand at him. As he looked, another clump of rocks hit his face, stinging his eyes. He yelped in pain and fear, and jumped back.

The humans approached, and suddenly one of them lobbed a larger rock. It hit his back, almost knocking him over and causing a sharp pain to radiate all the way down his leg. Realizing he was under attack, he took off, leaving the beach and vaulting over some logs. With a few more strides, he found himself in the forest. He paused to see if he was safe. The human voices seemed to be getting louder — were they following him? With no other choice, he began to follow a faint path deeper into the forest. Worried that it would lead him to Storm and her pack, he left the path and began to bushwhack his way through the dense undergrowth, tripping over sticks and getting scratched by sharp twigs. A moment later, he stopped again. All he could hear was the sound of his own breathing. The humans were not following him anymore.

He breathed a big sigh of relief, and turned to retrace his steps and find the path again. He had only taken a few steps when he heard a deep, menacing growl.

TWENTY
STORM

Scruff

"What are you doing in our forest?" Scruff saw a massive, silver-grey coyote emerging from the bushes where he had just come from — it must be Storm! Four other large coyotes flanked her, a silent and menacing army. Their hackles were raised, and they looked angry.

"Sorry — I was just ... I was just passing through. Quickly." His voice was shaky and came out as a squeak.

"You aren't allowed in this forest."

"I'm sorry — I'll leave right away." Scruff backed up slowly as he spoke, bumping into bushes as he tried to put some distance between himself and the coyotes.

"I don't know if that will be good enough. You are deep in our forest. You ignored our scent markings.

You have no right to be here and are not welcome." Her voice was low and menacing, and with each sentence she took a step toward him, the other coyotes following her like shadows.

Scruff knew without a doubt that there was no talking his way out of this one. Tucking his tail between his legs and flattening his ears, he turned and fled in the direction of the beach. The bushes were so thick that he could barely see. Branches scratched him and it was all he could do to avoid falling flat on his face. He heard howls and barks close behind him. At that moment, he stumbled on a rock, rolling over a few times. He immediately jumped up, but just as he did, one of the coyotes bit his tail, hard. Pain radiated through his body. He yelped and heard them laugh.

"Good one!"

"Keep running, runt!"

He raced on, his tail throbbing, and, with a few more bounds, broke out of the forest and onto a new beach. It wasn't busy, with just a few humans at one end of it. He heard them shout but didn't care. He could run faster here and he lengthened his stride until he reached the water's edge. Turning, he began to run along the shoreline, slowing slightly when he saw a large metal pipe ahead of him that lay across the beach and led into the water. Scruff arrived at it and tried to jump over it, but it was too high and his paws slipped off the metal. He had no chance. The five coyotes, right on his tail, stopped to form a semicircle around him, stalking closer. They blocked off the forest and the beach where they had come from, effectively cornering him. The large pipe was at his back and the only other exit was the ocean.

For a few seconds, they all stood there, sizing each other up. Then, with a growl, Storm launched herself toward him. He saw the large coyote descend, and quickly dove to the side, bumping into another coyote. This one jumped on top of him, and they tumbled over one another to the edge of the water. For a single second he was free, and he leapt in the only direction where there were no coyotes — straight into the waves. He moved deeper and deeper, the waves washing up against his chest. He could hear splashing behind him; he was still being pursued. He felt the icy cold of the water where he didn't have a thick coat to protect him. Pain radiated up his legs and he found it difficult to breathe.

He reached the point where he was so deep that his paws barely touched the ground and waves began to splash over his face, freezing water rushing into his ears. Breathing in water and beginning to choke, he turned around toward the beach again, desperately trying to escape the icy onslaught. He opened his eyes, and looked right into the sneering face of Storm, who lunged at him and bit him on the ear. He yelped, ripping his head away and launching himself farther into the water again.

He didn't know how his body knew what to do, but before he knew it his paws were scooping water in front of him, and he was afloat, moving slowly forward. He didn't dare look back. A wave rose up above him and he went under, but popped up again a second later. All he felt was cold water and his mouth was full of salt.

His lungs burned, and he found it more and more difficult to move his legs. His mouth was barely out of the water, and a wave crashed into his face, forcing water down his throat. Coughing hard, he lifted his nose desperately, trying to keep from inhaling more water. He almost headed back to shore, but, turning his head slightly, he saw five shapes slinking along, watching him. He couldn't do it. This was it. The way he was going to die.

But he willed his legs to keep moving. A few more minutes passed, and he was somewhat surprised to realize that he hadn't drowned yet. His swimming became slightly more efficient, and although he still couldn't feel his legs, his chest began to relax the tiniest bit, allowing him to get more air in each time. He still felt like he was on the edge of suffocating, coughing constantly as water sloshed into his mouth. A few minutes later, he realized that he had reached a new point of exhaustion, and sheer will was no longer enough. His legs began to slow down and he sank lower and lower in the water. His vision darkened. Without making a conscious decision, his brain made his body turn back toward the shore. He no longer cared if Storm was there. Eventually, one of his paws hit soft ground, and he was standing in chest-deep water. His head was low now and he coughed, trying to bring more air back into his lungs. A few seconds passed before his brain turned back on again, and he snapped his head up to see where he was.

Large rocks, covered in barnacles and seaweed, were strewn along the beach, and a long set of concrete stairs led the way up a steep, weedy embankment. There was a bad smell and he didn't see any humans or coyotes. Barely caring if Storm and her pack found him, he dragged himself up onto the rocks and collapsed.

TWENTY-ONE

HOME

Pica

Pica's journey back to the hillside went quickly. She only remembered bits and pieces of the landscape, and these memories were overlaid with pain. The scent of her family was long gone, but the oddest things brought back their memories vividly: Sage's big eyes the first time a train shrieked past them, Kai trying to balance on the railway ties, her mother's gentle tongue licking her wounds and encouraging her to keep going.

Travelling by herself for the first time in her life, she was acutely aware of the danger she was in. Not only was she not yet full-grown, but she didn't know this territory well. She kept her senses on alert for signs of another coyote, carefully skirting the boundaries when necessary.

Only a few hours had passed when she caught a scent that she recognized. She stopped short, her front paw hanging in the air, trying to place the smell. With a start, she realized that she was already back to the spot where her family had first joined the train track. The large industrial building on the left had a very distinctive chemical stench. She fully realized for the first time how injured she had been, and how slowly her family had travelled so that she could keep up with them. What had been going through Gree's mind on that journey? Had she ever considered leaving her behind? She shuddered, hoping that she would never be put in a situation like that. Her mother was so patient — she had never made Pica feel bad, despite the fact that the safety of her whole family had been compromised by her injury.

Lost in thought, she continued retracing her steps. She was still distracted when, at the edge of a dark park, she heard a high-pitched yipping howl close by. She froze. A few seconds later, she saw two shadows materialize out of the darkness. Two large coyotes, walking stiffly toward her, were showing signs of aggression. She crouched down submissively on the ground. Taking a deep breath, she called out, "I'm just passing through. I'm looking for my family." She took another breath, and then ventured, "Two females and three pups my age — have you seen them?"

"No. Move along," the male snapped, irritated. She glared at him — he hadn't even given it a thought. But when he took a step toward her, she thought better of trying to continue the conversation. She definitely wouldn't find her family if she let herself be attacked.

She continued on without event for another hour, her legs feeling quite tired now. She hadn't had much exercise over the last six weeks, and the lingering snow on the ground made travel a lot more difficult. As the cloudy sky began to lighten, she realized that it would be best for her to rest one more day, find something to eat and drink, and then attempt to find some more coyotes to ask about her family.

She looked for a place to sleep that no other coyote would want. Finding a busy road, she tucked herself under a clump of bushes on the side and dug into the ground. The sound of the traffic blocked out all other noises, and it smelled bad. She was fairly sure that no one would find her here.

She napped fitfully throughout the day, thoughts of Jagger swirling around in her mind. When the sky darkened again, she treaded carefully toward the hillside, stopping to eat some garbage from a back alley. It helped her hunger a little bit. She ate some snow, but knowing that it only quenched her thirst for a while, she kept her eyes out for puddles. As she travelled, she stayed alert for signs of other coyotes. It was risky, but she didn't know any other way to find her family. By the end of the night, she had found three other coyotes — a solitary male and a pair — but none of them had been helpful. They hadn't been overly aggressive, either, so she had gained more confidence in starting the conversations. She was about to give up and take a rest when she saw a dark shape at the end of an alley. She caught her breath and her heart felt like something was squeezing it tightly. It looked exactly like — but it couldn't be —

"Hi." The low bark sounded nothing like Jagger. She breathed out. His profile was similar — tall and lanky, fur not quite smooth. But his voice was completely different.

"Hi," she returned cautiously, stopping and waiting to see whether she should flee or not.

"I'm Patch," he offered, wagging his tail a little bit.

"Pica," she replied, not moving.

"What are you doing here?" In contrast to the aggression she was used to, Patch spoke in a neutral tone. He walked toward her unhurriedly, swinging his tail back and forth slowly. She noticed that his one dark ear did indeed look like a patch. He was younger than she had originally thought, probably born only a year or two before her.

"I'm just passing through, looking for my family." Pica took a few hesitant steps forward, cautiously sniffing him as they met.

"What do they look like?" he asked.

Pica hesitated. He seemed almost too friendly. But at least he was willing to take the time to consider her question. She described her family in detail, watching his face hopefully for a sign of recognition. He began nodding as she described Gree, and she broke off. "Do you know her?"

"I think so." He paused. "Haven't seen her around in a long time. But I haven't been in this area too much in the last little while. Why are you looking for them?"

Pica's heart sunk. It was not the lead she was hoping for. She tried to swallow, feeling emotion rise in her.

"Hey, are you okay?" The coyote seemed genuinely concerned. Pica couldn't stop herself. She told him her whole story, words spilling out of her. He just listened until she finished, a note of hopelessness in her voice.

Patch was quiet for a moment, looking sadly at her. "That's quite the story. I really hope you can find your family — I wish I could help you, but I'm pretty sure they haven't returned here." He paused, thinking. "I know Jagger, too, but I haven't seen him in a while, either."

Pica felt a bolt of electricity run through her. "What? Jagger is gone?"

"Well, ever since they demolished the hillside —"

"What?" Pica yelped.

"Oh, right, I guess you don't know about that. I think we're talking about the same hillside — right next to the golf course, right?"

"Yes. What happened?" Pica could hardly breathe.

"I think they're building some more houses there. Right now, there are just machines and temporary buildings there. Mostly I avoid it now, so I'm not sure what has been happening there lately."

Pica's face must have registered severe shock, because as Patch looked back at her, he quickly added, "Well, I'm not sure. You might want to go check it out. But either way, I do know Jagger, and I haven't run across him in a few weeks. I think it's quite possible that he moved on after the hillside was demolished."

Pica thought about this new information, unable to fully digest it. She couldn't even imagine the hillside not being there. She felt a rise of anger, thinking of how Jagger had torn apart her family, now all for nothing. It all seemed so senseless. She needed to see it for herself.

"Thanks for the information." She smiled at Patch. "Really, you are the first friendly coyote I've met around here."

"Thanks," he said, smiling at her. He walked over and laid his head gently on her back. "Maybe I can come with you?"

Her back suddenly felt hot and Pica jumped back. Was he looking for a partner? "Oh … well …" she stammered. "I wasn't … I didn't think …"

Patch just smiled. "Oh, it's okay. I can see you are still young and you need to figure some things out. I'm just saying, if I see you around again, we should talk some more." With a grin and a flick of his tail, he walked away down the alley.

Pica's mind swirled. The hillside gone — and Jagger maybe gone, too. And this new feeling, a funny fluttering in her stomach. She realized suddenly that time had been passing quickly, and she had grown into a much more adult body without even realizing it. First with fleeing Jagger, then getting captured, she had lost track of the fact that she was almost fully grown now. She would have to start thinking carefully when she was near male coyotes around her age.

She moved on, feeling something pulling her toward the hillside. She needed to find out what was happening there. She travelled cautiously, sniffing carefully for any signs of Jagger. She still couldn't believe that he might be gone. She finally made it to the edge of the busy road, and from there she could already tell that everything had changed. Breathing in the sharp, cold winter air, she smelled metal, fresh dirt, and oil. The sky was still dark, but she could make out the hulking shadows of the equipment against the sky. Carefully, she crossed the road and hopped the old rock barrier in order to find out more.

As she wandered around what used to be her hillside, she saw the extent of the damage. It had changed so much that she couldn't even find where her den site used to be. There were huge, gaping holes in the earth, and a wide gravel road that bisected the hillside. Machines rose everywhere from the newly turned earth, sinister in their stillness. The construction odours were so overpowering that they made her feel sick to her stomach, and she could detect very little else. The smells she had used as landmarks in the past were gone. Everything was ruined.

She began to feel overwhelmed and found herself climbing up the hill, trying to get some fresh air as she had done in the past so many times. Near the top, there was a small patch of ground that had not yet been touched. She used her nose to carefully pull out the various smells from her childhood. She picked out a sweet-smelling grass, a spicy one, and the smell of cold condensation on the earth. Then, at almost the same moment that she smelled him, she heard his voice.

"Well, well, well. Look who has dragged herself back home." The voice was unmistakable.

Pica whirled around. Standing behind her, up against the fence, was Jagger. She gasped — he looked terrible. His body was skinnier than it had ever been before, his ribs sticking out. His fur was patchy, and he had very little of it left on his tail. She shivered when they made eye contact. Despite his appearance, he still had his trademark sneering confidence.

"Jagger." She took a shaky breath. "I heard you were gone."

"I left when the machines moved in. But I still pass through this area from time to time, looking for …" He paused, looking directly at her with a smile. "… looking for food."

Pica began planning her escape route. She didn't know which direction would be best — Jagger was still faster and stronger than her and could probably catch her anywhere. He had killed her father; she was sure he wouldn't hesitate to kill her, too. She bunched up her muscles, preparing to run.

"I guess you're looking for your family," Jagger sneered.

Pica paused. "Do you know anything about them?"

"The idea that *I* would help a runt like *you* find your family. Ridiculous." Jagger threw back his head and laughed. "They certainly aren't around here anymore."

Pica felt the white-hot heat rising up in her, and she couldn't help herself. "No, Jagger, they aren't. Thanks to you. The way you and Scruff killed my father just to get the hillside — you ignored the code and showed yourself to be completely ruthless. And now, it seems that you are also completely stupid. You did it all for nothing." She jumped forward, landing squarely in front of him, propelled by her anger. "I hate you, and you deserve all of this — you're sick, and you have no home anymore. You deserve it all." She spat the words out.

He looked at her, anger suddenly sparking in his eyes. Raising himself to his full height, he responded between clenched teeth, "You'll regret saying that." They stood there, in a standoff, for a long moment, before she saw Jagger's muscles bunch up and she prepared herself for the attack.

TWENTY-TWO
CONFRONTATION

Scruff

When Scruff was able to open his eyes again, he looked around with relief. He was on a beach with no sign of humans or coyotes. There was an odd chemical smell in the air, making him feel sick to his stomach. He was not surprised that no one was here.

He knew he should move on, just in case Storm had followed him, but his body was too exhausted. He lay there unmoving until night fell. As the air cooled, he heard his stomach growl. Reluctantly, he dragged himself upright, and slowly climbed the staircase to leave the beach. He was surprised at how tired his leg muscles felt — they were twice as heavy as usual.

Above the beach was a neighbourhood with lots of houses, and he stayed on high alert, winding through backyards and alleys, making sure to stay still whenever he saw a human or a car. He tried to avoid other coyote markings, but was less cautious than usual — he was desperate for food and water. In one backyard, he scared a few birds away from a big basin filled with fresh water. It tasted a little bit mouldy, but he was so thirsty that he couldn't stop himself. He hoped it didn't make him feel sick later.

At the edge of a park, he found a pile of human garbage. It was old and smelled a little bit funny, but he ate it anyway. After, his stomach churned but he did feel better. For some reason, after all he'd been through, he felt an even stronger desire to get back to the hillside and confront Jagger. He had nothing left to lose. He didn't know exactly how to get back there, but was pretty sure he could retrace his steps to the hillside from the elevated train.

Scruff picked his way carefully through the different neighbourhoods, following familiar scents until he found the elevated train. From there, he began travelling back toward the hillside, taking detours to avoid other coyotes, and only travelling during the darkest part of the night. He made time to hunt as much as possible, feeling his strength slowly returning. However, his steady progress was halted when, halfway through the second night, he smelled something familiar. He was inspecting a pole at the entrance to a park to determine who had been there and how recently, when he caught a scent that smelled like Gree's. He frowned, and sniffed again, more carefully this time. It was unmistakable. She had been here many times, and quite recently. He looked around quickly, half expecting to see her loping toward him, a look of anger on her face. The street was dark and silent.

If Gree was here, then the rest of the pack must be here, too. He wanted more than anything else to avoid a confrontation. Retracing his steps, he moved away from the scent and spent the rest of the night making a wide, cautious arc to avoid the area. He went hours out of his way, carefully stopping to sniff at each major intersection to see if there were any more scent markings. The detour cost him an extra night, but it was worth it to avoid them. He didn't know what they would do if they saw him, but he didn't want to find out.

Finally, on the third night, he knew he was close. Things began to feel very familiar, and he picked up his pace. He stopped at a bush to inspect the smells, and was surprised to pick up a very familiar scent. Pica had been here very recently! He sniffed around, but didn't pick up on any other members of her pack. He frowned, confused. Why would she be here alone when her family was so far away? For a moment he hesitated, wondering whether to change his plans. But he had come so far, and felt unwilling to turn around without at least challenging Jagger. He pushed on, but more cautiously this time. He picked up Pica's scent a few more times. It was odd — it seemed that she, too, was heading for the hillside.

When he arrived at the edge of the hillside territory, he was immediately aware that it was not the same. The construction smells had never been so strong from this angle. He reached the road that bordered the hillside and, looking across it, was confronted by a field full of hulking metal machines and low buildings. He sat down in shock, staring blankly at the machines. He couldn't believe it. He felt his chest tense up and the flood of anger returned. After all that, the hillside was gone now, too. With less caution now, he galloped across the road, cleared the rock wall with a smooth leap, and trotted briskly through the construction site. His senses were trained on picking up any sign of Jagger. Would he still be here, or had he lost his chance to ever find out what had happened to his family?

If he climbed the hillside, he would have a better view of the whole area. Trotting up the hill, the dirt felt soft and cool against his paws. Being in the area again brought back memories. He was so caught up in thought that he missed hearing the conversation until he was almost right on top of them.

"No, Jagger." He heard Pica's voice, low with anger, "they aren't. Thanks to you. The way you and Scruff killed my father just to get the hillside — you ignored the code and showed yourself to be completely ruthless. And now, it seems that you are also completely stupid. You did it all for nothing." He heard a thump, and then she continued. "I hate you, and you deserve all of this — you're sick, and you have no home anymore. You deserve it all." She sounded furious.

Scruff took a few steps forward, coming around the side of a bush. There was Jagger, his body rigid, tufts of fur sticking out in all directions, standing face to face with Pica. Pica stood equally rigid, staring back at him.

He noticed that her body was larger now, her muscles long and lean. Neither of them noticed him.

Jagger stood straighter, taking a step toward Pica. "You'll regret saying that."

There was a beat as both coyotes prepared to spring toward one another. Then, before Scruff could react, he saw Jagger leap onto Pica, and Pica disappeared beneath him.

Almost before Scruff realized he was doing it, he growled and jumped around the bush, barrelling straight into Jagger. He knocked Jagger over and then fell over himself. Then, in a single breath, all three coyotes were on their feet and staring at each other in what was now a three-way standoff.

Jagger was the first to break the silence. He turned on Scruff with a snarl. "Nice to see you again, runt. Have you joined *her* side now?"

"I haven't joined anyone's side." Scruff tried to keep his voice low and controlled. He looked up, and almost stopped when his eyes met Jagger's two angry slits. He soldiered on. "It's just that every time I'm around you, someone is getting hurt. Lamar first, and now Pica? Haven't you harmed her family enough already? When will you just act like every other coyote and leave well enough alone?" As he spoke, he sensed Pica turn to look at him, but he felt unable to meet her eyes.

"She was the one who came back," Jagger snarled, indicating Pica. "She's trespassing."

"Trespassing on what land? This hole of a construction site?" Scruff hurled back. "You would hurt Pica to defend this?"

Jagger stared him down for a long minute. "You should have stayed away, after what you did."

"After what *I* did?" Scruff's anger fuelled him to speak more recklessly than he ever had before to Jagger. "You were the one who lied to convince me to help you kill Lamar. You used me. Did you lie to me about my parents, too? You killed them, didn't you? It makes sense. You wanted the forest, and you were conveniently right there after they died. I wish you had just killed me, too."

Scruff paused for a breath. He hadn't expected all that to come out.

Before Jagger could respond, Pica jumped in, turning to him with intensity. "You were a pup from the Forest Pack? I never knew that!"

"You runts really have no idea," Jagger scoffed. "No idea at all."

"No idea of what, Jagger?" Pica replied angrily. "No idea of what happened to Scruff's parents? Actually, I do. I overheard my parents talking about it, and they said *you* had killed coyotes before. It seems pretty clear to me."

"Tell me." Scruff looked deep into Jagger's eyes, feeling a little dizzy. "You owe me the truth."

Jagger looked between them for a moment, and slowly he began to chuckle. The chuckle turned into a laugh, and right in front of their eyes, he began to belly-laugh uncontrollably. Scruff and Pica just stared at him, not comprehending. Finally, he paused to take a breath.

"Scruff, you can believe whatever you want. It's all screwed up, anyway. I tried my best to help you, but I'm done with all of this." He shook his head slowly and turned around, smoothly slipping under the fence. Scruff could hear the soft padding as he loped away. As he stood there, feeling confused, he became more aware of the body breathing slowly beside him. The cold winter sun had just lifted above the hillside, and when he finally turned to look at her, he saw she was staring back at him with an unreadable expression. He quickly dropped his eyes and turned away, unsure of what to do or what to say. Of all of the outcomes he had thought might come from his return to the hillside, this was far away from any of them.

Pica

Pica watched as Scruff walked away slowly from her, his head hung low, sitting down on the hillside a short distance away. His back to her, he looked out over the construction site and the golf course. His body was still small for a coyote, but his muscles had filled out and he looked tougher. The conversation with Jagger kept running through her head. Now that she thought about it, of course Scruff wouldn't have known who killed his parents — he wouldn't have been so tight with Jagger if he had. Looking at him, she couldn't help but shiver, thinking about how he had helped to kill her father. How had Jagger lied to him to make him do that? She needed to know more.

She cast a nervous glance back at the fenceline. Could Jagger have been lying again so he could catch them unawares? It was possible, but she didn't think that in his state, looking skinny and malnourished, he would willingly take on the two of them. Although neither she nor Scruff was full-grown, they were strong. Together they would have a good chance at injuring him. He couldn't afford to risk it. She figured they were likely safe for now.

She padded over softly and sat next to Scruff. Close, but not too close. She found it difficult to look at him. Looking at him made her think about her father and that terrible night. She gazed out over the hillside, avoiding having to look him in the eyes.

It was quiet for a few moments, and then Scruff broke the silence. "Pica, I'm sorry." His voice was almost inaudible.

"I never knew all of that before — where you came from and who your parents were."

"I was so little when my parents died that I don't really remember much. After my siblings died, Jagger saved me for some reason. I still don't understand why."

Pica frowned. "What did he tell you about your parents?"

"Well," Scruff paused for a second, "he told me that Lamar killed them."

"What?" Pica burst out, snapping her head around to glare at him.

He looked up to make brief eye contact, then quickly looked away. "He told me that Lamar and Gree needed more space with you and everyone else, and they were trying to expand their territory."

"But that's ridiculous — we had the whole hillside!"

"I didn't know any better. I think he just wanted to make me hate you."

"I guess that's why you helped him kill ..." Pica couldn't quite finish the sentence.

"I didn't know that he was going to do that. If I could go back and change things, I would. But I can't. I came back because I needed to know that truth. Now I can go."

Pica paused, considering. "I can see how you would believe him. He kind of had control over you, you know. It's hard when you are young — it was the same with us, I guess. We just believed whatever our parents told us, too."

"Well, in the end, he just used me. He destroyed my life, and yours. And the lives of your family. Wait — why aren't you with your family?" Scruff finally looked up at her, his soft brown eyes registering confusion.

Pica smiled sadly. "It's a long story."

Scruff nodded his head toward the rising sun. "We have a while."

"I guess so." Pica launched into her story, starting from the moment when Scruff warned them to get away from the hillside. She detailed her injury, their flight, and getting captured. Scruff kept interrupting her to ask questions about her time at the rehabilitation centre. It was hard for her to describe it, because she had nothing to compare it to. She finally got to the point of her release and decision to return to the hillside to find out where her family was.

"Pica." Scruff looked at her intently. "I know where they are."

Pica stared at him. "What?"

"On my way here I smelled Gree and a few of your siblings. It was recent. They might have been passing through, but even if so, I'm sure we can track them from there."

Pica's heart was racing. She could hardly believe him. "You're sure?"

"It was unmistakable."

She jumped up, feeling suddenly euphoric. "We have to go now! I can't believe it! How far are they — how long will it take? Why didn't you tell me sooner? Where were you when you smelled them? Can we find them today?"

Scruff grinned. "Sorry — at first I had no idea you didn't know where they were. Then, I got caught up in your story. I can help you find them, but it's a bit of a trip. It took me two nights."

"Two nights?" Pica felt deflated. "Well, if we travel through the day, we could —"

"There is no sense in getting killed just to get there a little faster," Scruff cut in. "Why don't we wait for dusk, and then we'll travel as far as we can overnight. Tomorrow we can rest, and I bet we can make it there the second night."

"I don't know if I can wait," Pica declared.

"Well, if you have to go, we can go now. But the area around here is pretty busy in the day. I don't think it would be worth it."

Pica sighed. "Fine. But this day is going to pass so slowly."

"I can help pass the time," Scruff said, grinning at her. "Why don't I tell you about when a pack of huge coyotes chased me into the ocean and I almost drowned?"

Pica stared at him intently, her interest piqued. "What's an ocean? And why were you near a pack of huge coyotes?" Inviting him to follow her, she trotted over to a dip in the hillside where they would be out of sight of all the humans arriving for work. "Fine. We'll lie here for the day and you can entertain me with stories." She laid her body out on the grass, and felt Scruff lie down next to her. For a moment, she had a flash of apprehension, as she remembered who this was lying next to her. Was he really who he said he was? Could he truly not have known? She frowned, and put it out of her mind. Either way, he was going to help her find her family, so it didn't really matter for now.

TWENTY-THREE

TEAMWORK

Pica

The day passed slowly for Pica. After talking to Scruff for a few hours, her eyes began to close, and she realized that she was exhausted. They tried to nap in the grass, but the noise from the construction site constantly disrupted them, and they ended up retreating to a shed behind a house on the other side of the fence.

It was quieter in the shed, but there, thoughts of Jagger resurfaced. It was clear that he didn't live in the hillside area anymore, but Pica knew that he and Scruff used to live in an abandoned house not far from here. Could he still be there? They decided to take turns staying alert, watching for danger.

In between naps, they talked some more. Scruff seemed eager to talk to her, but she still wasn't sure how she felt about him. Now that she understood more about his past, she felt sorry for him. She could understand how he could have ended up being there when Jagger killed Lamar. However, a part of her still couldn't quite forgive him. He may not have known it was about to happen, but he hadn't done anything to stop it. He may not be a monster, but he was not a friend, either.

As soon as dusk began to fall, she jumped up and stretched. Scruff opened one eye, and then closed it again. "Come on, Pica, wait a little longer. I can still see the shadows."

"Shadows? There are absolutely no shadows around!" She was impatient. Clearly, he did not share the urgency that she felt. Her family was out there somewhere, and only he could help her find them. She jumped over to him and pushed at his body with her nose. Then she batted his tail with her paws. "Scruff, let's go! We'll be careful."

Scruff yawned and stood slowly. "Fine." He looked at her, shaking his head and smiling a little bit. "I get it — it's important. I don't know what they'll do when they see you!"

"Well, I do." Pica felt a warm feeling spread from her chest through her whole body. She could picture the scene in her head. Dane bounding over, Kai's yelp of surprise, Sage's warm eyes, and her mom, the relief evident. Reluctantly, she broke out of her reverie and looked over at Scruff. He had turned away from her and looked upset.

"What's wrong?"

"Nothing. Let's go." Scruff trotted off down the alley, not waiting to see if she would follow.

Pica felt irritated as she trotted behind him. After everything he had done to break up her family, he didn't seem that eager to help her. However, as they travelled, she calmed down a little bit. He really was in a tough situation — he clearly didn't want any future with Jagger, and her family would probably try to kill him if they saw him. Even though her family wasn't aware of all she had learned about him, it didn't change the fact that he had been present when her father was killed. After leading her back to her family, Scruff would have no choice but to go back to the city alone. She felt a sadness well up in her — she knew what it was like to feel lonely. The feeling sat with her for a moment before she shook it off. There was nothing she could do about it. It was his problem, not hers.

Scruff kept up a quick pace. They stopped for water, but didn't take the time to hunt. She was impressed at how Scruff navigated the busy neighbourhood. Here, houses were denser, and Pica often didn't see any green space. Scruff melted into the shadows on the street in front of her, freezing if a car passed, and if she wasn't following him carefully, she found it quite difficult to find him in the darkness. She began to mimic him, and when a large, noisy group of humans walked past them, they simply froze. Even with nothing to hide them, and only a few feet between them and the humans, they weren't detected. Pica wondered how humans were so strong when they seemed to have no senses at all.

By the time the first rays of morning light broke across the dark grey sky, Pica was ready to stop. Her paws ached, and she was very hungry. They slept the day away, out of sight of the humans in a small shed, and when darkness came again, Pica jumped up, stretching her aching muscles. "All right — let's go. But I need to find some food."

"Me, too," Scruff agreed. They travelled more slowly at first, moving up the street, one on either side, senses on alert, looking for food. They came to a busy street, and Scruff showed her where, in the alley around the back of the buildings, there were lines of delicious-smelling Dumpsters. He motioned her to be silent, and they approached the Dumpster slowly. Within seconds, Pica had located a rat and, as it moved in front of her, leaped toward it. It swerved away from her but ran straight into Scruff, who snatched it with a quick pounce.

"Nice work, Pica! That was awesome."

Pica grinned. It hadn't been her intention to do that, but it was effective. Scruff shared the meat, and although small, it tasted delicious and whetted her appetite for more. They found some human food in a small container beside the Dumpster, but it tasted spicy and made her cough. They worked together to kill another rat at the next Dumpster they came to. This time, Scruff scared it toward Pica, and she pounced on it, nervous that she would miss. When she felt the small body under her paws, she yelped with joy. It felt wonderful to make a real kill, and to be able to share it with Scruff.

"Good teamwork!" yipped Scruff from where he was standing a few metres away.

"That worked pretty well," said Pica, smiling. It was interesting that, in the hunting lessons her parents had given her, they had always stressed the importance of solo hunting. She now saw how hunting with two or more coyotes could have a real advantage, and wondered why she had never hunted in a team with her siblings. It was fun, and easier, too.

"Lots of coyotes hunt in pairs," said Scruff, reading her mind as he dug into the food. "It's just that you have to be able to hunt alone, just in case. But it can be a real advantage to work together."

"Did you learn that with Jagger?"

"No. He wasn't a big fan of hunting with anyone else. But I've seen other coyotes hunting together."

"How did you learn to hunt in the first place?"

"Oh, Jagger did teach me how to hunt. But we never went anywhere as a team, you know?" Scruff's voice was wistful.

"That's too bad. I went hunting with my family all the time. But it was hard — I could never catch anything because of my eye. But when I was captured and went to that place, I got lots of hunting practice, and I think I'm doing a lot better now."

"What's wrong with your eye?"

Pica looked up at him, surprised, realizing that he hadn't known or noticed. "Something happened when I was younger, and now I can't see out of one of my eyes. That's why I always had so much trouble hunting, I think."

"Oh. Well, it seems like you're doing fine now," Scruff replied encouragingly.

"I hope so. I haven't really had the chance to see how much I've improved yet."

They continued to eat in silence for a few minutes until the aching hunger had worn off. Pica groaned, feeling her full belly. "I think I need a rest before I can go on."

"You, who never wants to stop?" teased Scruff with a smile.

"Come on — could you run right now?"

"I guess not. Okay, let's find a spot to rest for a bit, and then we'll continue. I think we can get there tonight, especially now that we aren't so hungry."

They wandered around until they found some soft dirt under a few trees in the corner of someone's backyard. They couldn't smell any other animals around, and the house was dark and silent. Pica curled up with a sigh of relief, letting her stomach swell out. Scruff curled up beside her, his head and neck pressed lightly against her back. She stiffened and felt him immediately move away. "Sorry," he said quietly.

"It's okay." Pica didn't really know what to say. She felt cold, and the idea of being able to share heat was very appealing. The last week had been a little warmer, but tonight the air felt frosty and there was a wind that ruffled her fur, pushing cold air up against her skin. She waited a few minutes, shivering, until the idea of warmth became too tempting. She slowly moved to curl up against him, feeling the heat from his body relaxing her. She fell asleep almost immediately.

TWENTY-FOUR

TRUTH

Pica

When Pica woke, her stomach was feeling normal again, and she stood and stretched, immediately missing the feeling of the warm body next to her. Without the shared heat, she quickly began to cool off. Scruff, next to her, jumped up.

"Hey." He looked at her and smiled.

"Hey." Pica couldn't quite bring herself to smile back. She felt a little bit embarrassed about having curled up so close to him, and didn't know how to act. She tried to meet his eyes but found it difficult. She took off down the alley, calling out behind her, "Okay, let's go then."

They loped through neighbourhood after neighbourhood, Scruff somehow knowing where he was going. He was obviously trying to take as direct a route as possible, but sometimes they had to detour because of strange smells or busy roads. The streets all seemed so similar to Pica, with dense apartment buildings that rose high above the streets. There was much more night activity than she was used to near the golf course, and she couldn't figure out how other coyotes could make a home here. Where did they sleep? How did they deal with the constant noise? She felt sad, thinking of how the hillside where she grew up would never be home to another coyote family.

She noticed Scruff's focus intensify as they began to make right-angle turns, double back, and walk in wide circles. "Are we close?" Pica called as he dashed across the street, following a smell.

"Yes. I know we're close to the park where I smelled them. I just can't quite remember where it was."

They continued circling and were travelling down another nondescript street when something made Pica stop in her tracks. It was Dane. He had been here recently. She located the scent along a horizontal metal bar that marked the side of the stairs. She yelped in excitement and Scruff trotted over to smell it, too.

"We found them!" Pica couldn't keep the excitement out of her voice.

"Yes. But the scent isn't that fresh — we'll need to fan out to figure out where they came from." Scruff sounded less excited.

"All right." Pica was frustrated because the smell was too old to know what direction Dane had been travelling. But even without this information, she couldn't help but feel optimistic. She was sure they would pick up the trail soon. The first few directions they tried didn't work, but when they left the road and headed downhill toward a cluster of low-lying apartment buildings, they had their first hit.

"Right here," Scruff called out, sniffing a post, and continuing on down the hill. They passed into a small industrial area. A few long, low buildings lined the streets, and there were patches of forest and bushes behind them. Scruff and Pica fanned out, each trying to find a recent scent mark. Pica looked up at the sky — there wasn't much time left if they were going to find them before daybreak.

Then, suddenly, from the other side of a chain-link fence came the muted but unmistakable sound of Sage's happy hunting yip. Without even realizing it, Pica sent out a long return howl, running along the fenceline, looking for a way through. For a moment, she didn't hear anything, and then a chorus of yips and howls rang out loudly through the dawn. She saw three furry bodies tearing around the side of the building, and she yipped even louder as she recognized her family. She threw herself against the fence as Dane, Sage, and Gree approached from the other side, whining and licking at them through the wire mesh.

"Pica!"

"I can't get through!"

"Where were you?"

"How did you find us?"

"Where is everyone else?"

They all talked at once and over top of each other, when suddenly Gree stilled and stepped away. Her fur went up, and her stance abruptly shifted to a much more aggressive pose. Looking over Pica's shoulder, a deep growl ripped out of her.

"You."

Pica looked over her shoulder, and saw Scruff standing a short distance away, his body position submissive, looking at them with wide eyes.

"Mom, listen. It's Scruff. He helped me —"

"I know who he is," Gree cut her off. "Your father's killer." She left Pica and began galloping down the fence-line. Pica knew she was heading for somewhere where she could get through. And as soon as she did, she would attack Scruff. "No! Stop!" she screamed as her mother squeezed under the fence. Gree stood up and shook out her fur. She was fierce — tall, with lean, strong chest muscles and a long, pointed muzzle. Seeing Scruff running away, she leapt toward him in pursuit.

"Mom — stop!" Pica leapt directly in front of her, feeling the full force as Gree ran directly into her, bowling her over. Pica couldn't get any more words out, unable to breathe from the impact. Gree stopped and turned, looking at her with surprise. She looked around for Scruff, but not seeing him, took a few steps to return to Pica.

"Pica — what was that all about?"

"It's ... I need to ..." Pica couldn't get the words out.

"Take a second. Breathe." Sage was beside her now, her body pressing against Pica's. Pica saw Taba come around the side of a building with Kai, and they also scraped under the fence to cover Pica with kisses. Then they just stood there together. Pica soaked up the feeling of being with her family again. She could feel their eyes on her as she struggled to regain her breath. Finally, she was able to speak.

"You can't attack Scruff — he helped me. When I was back at the hillside, I ran into him —"

"How did you end up back at the hillside?"

"What happened to you?"

"Are you okay?"

Everyone in her family interrupted Pica at the same time. Then they all stopped and Gree laughed. "Clearly, we have a lot of catching up to do. For now, we'll show you where we're living. It's already light and we can't stay here. We'll talk about everything." She glanced at the direction where Scruff had disappeared and her eyes narrowed suspiciously. "You can tell us what you want to say about Scruff, but I can't promise not to go after him tomorrow night."

Pica followed her family back through the fence and to a small ravine situated between two of the industrial buildings. It was a good spot — quiet and out of the way, with no paths or roads running through it and a creek trickling down the middle of it. They all tucked in under a large tree and began to talk.

Pica began by explaining what happened to her after they had left her in the schoolyard. Everyone stared at her with wide eyes. Her parents had heard about coyotes being captured by humans, but had never talked to anyone who had lived through it. Her siblings were amazed.

Kai kept interrupting her to ask more about one detail or another. Eventually, Sage sighed impatiently. "Enough with the details! What happened to you once you got free, Pica? How did you get back here?"

Pica told them everything about returning to the hillside to look for them and running into Jagger in the new construction site. She tried not to leave anything out, and her family listened intently.

When she stopped, Gree spoke up. "I can't quite believe it. It's a miracle you are here." She nuzzled Pica gently, giving her face a good lick. "And you are right, Scruff is a bit of a complicated situation. I guess we might have misunderstood his relationship with Jagger. That is a surprise to me — they always seemed so close."

"Well, I don't know how it happened, but I like him now," Pica replied. "I believe him — I don't think he meant to help Jagger kill Dad, and even if he did, well, Jagger told him that you guys killed his parents. So he was kind of messed up."

Gree and Taba exchanged glances. Neither of them spoke for a moment, but they communicated something silently. Pica looked at her siblings, who returned her puzzled glance, also sensing something weird.

"What? What are you looking at each other like that for?"

"Nothing," Gree said gently. "It just sounded like you were taking his side, Pica. You know that he and Jagger are our enemies."

Pica bristled. "I don't see why Scruff has to be our enemy. He is nice, and —"

Gree interrupted her, snapping, "And what, Pica? You think we should welcome him into our pack? We barely have enough land for us. You're forgetting that the pack comes first, no matter what."

"He is a good hunter, though, and he's strong." Pica wasn't sure why she was suddenly defending him. She just felt mad that her mother wasn't even giving him a chance.

"All that matters is the pack." Gree's tone was final.

"But …" Pica couldn't stop herself, even though she saw Dane giving her a look. "But, it doesn't mean we have to hate everyone else, does it? I'm not talking about Jagger, but —"

"You don't know what you are talking about!" Taba cut her off angrily. Gree shot her a look that told her to stay out of it.

Gree took a long breath. "Pica, you're right, we don't have to hate everyone else. But it's complicated. There are some things that we never told you."

"Like what?" Kai popped in. He was following every word.

"Well …" Gree paused. Her face was serious now. "A lot of what Jagger told Scruff was true. Our family *is* large, and we did need more land for all of you. The hillside wasn't big enough unless you all left as soon as you were old enough. Your father and I wanted to make a bigger and stronger pack, so that we would never have to worry about being challenged there."

Pica glanced at Dane. He caught her glance, and his expression told her that he had no idea about this, either.

Gree continued, "The Forest Pack was standing in our way. Scruff was born to them the same year you were, along with other pups. Their pack was growing, too, and not only did they occupy the land we wanted, but we were worried that they would want to expand to the hillside." She paused, looking into each of their eyes to make sure they were following. With conviction in her voice, she continued, "You need to understand that Jagger was telling Scruff the truth. He didn't kill the Forest Pack. We did."

There was a stunned silence. Pica could barely breathe. None of her siblings moved a muscle.

"What?" Pica finally got a single syllable out. Her mouth had dried up and she couldn't even swallow.

Gree made direct eye contact with her, her eyes soft. "It's not as bad as you think. We never intended to kill them, just run them off the land and force them to go elsewhere. We wanted more land, but not at the expense of getting injured in a vicious fight. But the spring when you were born, Scruff's father got sick. We saw big chunks of his fur falling out, and we could see all of his ribs. Then he disappeared — went somewhere to die, we figured. We saw that Scruff's mother was sick, too, probably with the same thing. And this was our opportunity. They were all going to die, and another coyote was going to just come along and step into that space. But if we were there when she died, we could immediately claim the forest for our family."

"What?" Pica repeated, her voice a squeak. She heard blood pumping loudly in her ears. She could barely follow all of the details.

"Once she — Scruff's mother — was too weak to run, we decided it was time to force her out. We knew the pups were as good as dead — I don't think they had been getting enough food all along. One night, we left you all with Taba and went to challenge her. She was out hunting, and knowing what we were up to, tried to return to the den area. We cut her off and she panicked. I don't think she even looked when she crossed the street — a truck hit her and killed her."

"No." Pica heard her voice quiver with anger. "A truck didn't kill her — *you* killed her. You're a murderer — and so was Dad!" She jumped up, furious. "How could you lie to us? All this time you blamed Jagger —"

"We never blamed Jagger." Gree's tone was sharp. "All we said was that he was a dangerous coyote — and he is. Dangerous to our family. And look at how he treated Scruff, his own brother — he should have treated him much better. Pica —"

"Wait — what?" Pica broke in. "How are they brothers?"

Gree sighed. "I guess you never knew that, either. Jagger was born to the Forest Pack a few years back. Something bad happened — I'm not entirely sure what — but his parents drove him away when he was only five months old. We didn't see him again until after they died."

As Gree paused, Pica realized that she wasn't breathing. Taking in a huge gasp of air, she tried to steady herself. "Why didn't you tell us any of this before?"

"Pica, we needed to protect our family. None of those details are really important — all you needed to know was that they were both potentially dangerous and to stay away. Lamar and I regretted not fighting off Jagger when he first arrived. He showed up soon after Scruff's mother died, and he was so aggressive that Lamar was worried about injuring himself in a face-to-face confrontation. It is rare to receive that kind of challenge from a lone coyote, but with you pups so little, our pack was weak. Someone always needed to be back guarding you, and I was especially weak, having just given birth. We decided to let him have the forest and hopefully we would be able to run him off later, when you were all older. Obviously, that was the wrong decision. If we had challenged him earlier, your father would still be alive, and we would still be living on the hillside." Her voice shook with sadness.

Taba walked over to where Gree was standing, her head bowed, and nosed her back. "You didn't let us down. You always did the best you could."

Taba then walked over to where Pica was standing, shell-shocked. She nosed her gently. "Hey — Pica. Think about it. That's the way it works. It's our pack against the world."

"And so we killed a mother and sentenced her pups to death?"

"They would have died anyway."

"But they didn't — Scruff survived when Jagger saved him."

"Jagger only saved him so he could use him. He's worse than us."

Pica shook her head, disbelieving. She looked at Sage. "Sage? Did you know?"

Sage looked back at her with sad eyes. "No, I didn't. But I get it. They were just trying to protect us."

Something in Pica snapped. She whirled around, looking from family member one to another. "I think it's stupid. All of this. Killing other coyotes, abandoning pups. All for what? To steal a little patch of trees?"

"That little patch of trees was necessary to maintain our family." Gree spoke sharply. "*Our* family, Pica. The pack who raised you, protected you. Scruff is not our family. He should have died a long time ago."

"I can't believe you would say that." Pica felt the anger driving her, causing her to back away from her family. She couldn't believe what she was hearing. All along, she had believed that Jagger had killed Scruff's family. She had tried to convince Scruff of it, too. Where was he now? What was he doing?

She turned, taking a few steps away. "I have to tell him. He deserves to know the truth."

Gree stood and blocked her path. "Pica, telling him the truth won't give him any peace. Just let him go — this is your family, right here. You don't need to save him."

Pica shook her head, stepping around her mother. "No, you're wrong. I *do* have to tell him. He saved me, and I never thanked him. He helped me come back to you. I owe it to him to let him know the truth."

Gree sighed, her eyes softening. "At least wait until dark."

"I can't wait. I can't let him get too far away or I'll never find him again!" Her voice was choked with emotion.

"Fine." Gree stepped aside. "I can't stop you. But be careful, and come back safe. We just found you. I love you."

Pica looked at her family one more time, feeling conflicted, and then turned, retracing her steps back to the fence where she had last seen Scruff.

TWENTY-FIVE
PACK

Scruff

After leaving Pica, Scruff hadn't made it that far. The streets were barely illuminated by the blue morning light, and he was vaguely aware of cars honking at him as he wound through the streets, looking for a place to lie down. He just wanted to curl up somewhere dark, close his eyes, and block out the world. Eventually, he passed a small park. The trash can was tipped over and small scraps of garbage were strewn across the grass, picked over by crows, pigeons, and other small animals. He sniffed briefly — nothing edible remained. Something in the can smelled sharp and acrid, making his nose burn.

He almost continued, but then, seeing a low bush behind the toppled container, realized that this would be the perfect cover. No one would smell him over the trash odours. He would be left alone, which was all he wanted now. He dug into the cold dirt, frozen chunks cracking off of the ground, and curled up deep under the bush. His nose slowly began to stop stinging, and he became more aware of the cold ground against his body. He shivered, pushing his nose underneath his tail.

He thought back to the last few days. He had finally confronted Jagger, but still didn't really understand why Jagger had taken him in. It was clear to him now that Jagger was bitter and violent, having killed his family and likely others, but why he had spared Scruff and raised him was still a mystery. He would probably never know. He felt a little bit comforted knowing that he had been able to help Pica find her family again. At least now they were together. It was the least he could do.

Picturing them together gave him a sudden pang of loneliness. The last few days had been so nice, being with Pica. She was someone he could talk to, hunt with, and even laugh with. His time with her had been so different than anything he had experienced before. He had been lonely his whole life, but he had never felt as alone as he did now.

He would never go back to the hillside, and he couldn't go anywhere near Pica's family. He didn't really want to go back to his spot under the train in the heart of the city, either; it was a lonely, noisy place. There had to be something better. He thought then of what the old coyote Mala had said when he met her on the beach. She had talked about the Wild Lands on the other side of the bridge, different but full of opportunity. Fewer people, and more space. Even though she had said it was difficult to survive there, the idea appealed to him. It would be a true fresh start. He wouldn't worry about running into anyone from his past.

He dozed lightly through the day, the cold preventing him from falling into a deep sleep. At some point in the middle of the day, a noise caught his attention. Removing his nose reluctantly from the warm pocket his body had made for it, he looked up. Through the branches, he could see a slim grey shadow walking slowly on the other side of the park. He recognized Pica immediately, and his heart gave a jump. What was she doing here? He was immediately alert. He almost called out to her, but then he hesitated. What if her family was nearby?

He longingly watched her cross through the park and begin to round the corner out of sight. A few moments passed, and then he couldn't stand it any longer. He had to know why she was here. Standing up, he gave a low bark, then another one, louder, to make sure it was heard over the background sound of the cars on the roads surrounding the park. A few moments later, he saw her re-emerge from behind the bushes at the corner of the park. He rose slowly and came out from under the bush. Pica spotted him and stopped. For a few moments, they just stared at one another across the park. Then, Pica put her ears back in happiness and ran over to him.

"Scruff!" she exclaimed as she got close, nudging him with her nose.

"What are you doing here?" he asked, taken aback by her friendliness.

"It's a long story." She paused, her nose wrinkling. "What are you doing near this terrible-smelling pile of garbage?"

He smiled, realizing that it was a bit odd. "I didn't want other coyotes to find me. It seemed safe."

They stood for a moment, just staring at one another. Scruff tried to hide his delight at seeing her again. For some reason he didn't want her to know how lonely he had been feeling.

"Well," Pica ventured, "my nose isn't really getting used to this stench. Why don't we go to the other side of the park? I have to talk to you about something."

Intrigued, Scruff followed her across the park to another clump of bushes. He sat down and looked at her. She stayed standing, shifting her weight from side to side. He couldn't quite read her expression, but he could tell she was nervous and began to worry about what she was about to say.

"What's up, Pica?"

"Well, I have some things to tell you." Her voice was low and serious, and he felt fear grip his stomach. His mind started racing — what could be bad enough that she would come and find him to tell him? Unless, of course, Jagger was back and had hurt someone else?

She continued slowly and carefully. "I don't know how to tell you this, but you deserve to know. You might hate me and my family when I'm done, and I would understand that. But it's not right that you should leave without the truth."

Scruff frowned, now very confused. What could she possibly say that would make him mad at her?

"It's hard to start … I guess I should just get it out. I talked with my family this morning and told them about our confrontation with Jagger, and how you saved me from an attack. Then I told them about how he had lied to you about my father killing your parents." She paused, gathering her thoughts. "Scruff, this is going to be a big surprise to you, but Jagger didn't lie to you about killing your parents. He was terrible to you, but I know for sure now that he didn't kill them."

Scruff frowned. "I don't understand. If he didn't, then who did?"

Pica's face crumpled. She looked miserable. Staring at the ground, she answered him. "It was my family."

"What?" Scruff's mind went blank, trying to process this new information.

"My mom told me this morning that your father was very sick and died of an illness. Then it was just you, your mother, and your siblings. You must have been tiny, still in the den — and then your mom got sick, too. My parents decided to run her off the territory to get more room for my family. They chased her until she got hit by a car."

Scruff was silent. He had always had a deep longing to know in more detail what happened to his parents, but hearing about it made him feel their deaths more sharply, as if it were happening all over again. He looked at Pica, still not quite comprehending. "So he was telling me the truth all along. It was your family who was lying."

Pica didn't make eye contact with him. "I'm so sorry," she said, her voice low. "I didn't know any of this." She paused, taking a shaky breath. "And ... there is some more."

Scruff waited, his head down. He didn't know if he wanted to hear anything else.

"Scruff, my mom also told me that Jagger is your brother from a previous litter. You share the same parents."

Scruff looked up at this, his breath catching. "What? Are you sure?"

"I don't know why she would lie about it. I think she recognized his scent from before."

"But why wouldn't he tell me? And why would he be so mean? I don't understand."

"This is all new to me, too. I don't know why he used you like he did. And I don't know why neither of us found out until now. But now you know. Although I'm not sure it helps."

They were both silent for a few minutes. Images of Scruff's life flashed through his head: Jagger punishing him, feeling lonely and ignored for days at a time, Jagger's cool smile after he had killed Lamar. Finally, he spoke. "You're right, it doesn't help. He's not my family — he's nothing to me. I have nothing. And now the last few threads keeping my life together are broken." Feeling the darkness seep into him, he turned his back to her and curled up in a ball.

"Scruff," Pica began, her voice tentative.

He buried his nose deeper under his tail. "I don't want to talk about it anymore." He closed his eyes tight. He heard a few footsteps and then she was gone.

Pica

Pica's head hurt. She had hoped to give Scruff some relief in knowing the truth, but now he was so much more miserable than before. Gree was right, he probably would have been better off not knowing. It felt terrible to leave him so hopeless.

She crossed the park, ducking out of the way when some small humans appeared in front of her on the path. She heard them shout and picked up her pace, heading away from the park. She crossed the street and then entered a quiet front yard, needing time to think.

The thing that surprised her the most was that Scruff hadn't even seemed angry. Maybe that was the worst part — it would have been easier to leave if he had yelled at her or insulted her family. Instead, he looked like he had just given up. She didn't blame him. He didn't have anyone looking out for him in his life. At least she knew that she always had others who loved her.

Looking back, she realized that she had been sheltered. She had never questioned how her family had come to live on such a beautiful and desirable piece of land; in fact, it wasn't until she saw the rest of the city that she truly appreciated her home. She had grown up thinking that the world was simple. Her parents were good and loved their pups, and the main challenge in life was to find enough food. Now, she was starting to understand that the relationships between coyotes were complex, and there were difficult decisions that had to be made to protect the pack. Anger toward her family began to melt away. Her parents weren't perfect, but they had done everything they could to support Pica and her siblings while they were growing up.

And then there was Scruff. As she lay quietly, letting the day pass by, her thoughts kept returning to him. Considering all of the obstacles in his life, he had turned out surprisingly well. Travelling with him for those few days had been fun. He was funny and thoughtful, and he had turned into an excellent hunter. He'd had a tough life, but his personality didn't reflect it.

When the sun finally went down and the streets were bathed in a dusky grey, Pica rose, stretching. As she reached the sidewalk, she knew exactly where she was going. She felt the wind lifting her fur up, the cold air making her skin feel almost electrified. The palette of nighttime greys around her was muted but beautiful.

It was only moments until she was there. She saw him, still curled up in a ball, right where she had left him. Without hesitation, she walked over to him softly and lay down beside him, curling up against him. She felt him jolt awake and take a few quick breaths. Then he became completely still. She had a moment of doubt, wondering whether he would leave. A second later, he pressed up against her and shared his warmth. She breathed out and smiled. This was where she was needed to be.

They didn't talk for a few hours, enjoying the feeling of warm fur and sides moving together in breath. Eventually, Scruff stretched out and sat up, looking at her curiously.

"So."

She opened her eyes and glanced at him. "So."

He raised his eyebrows. She sighed, admitting, "I'm joining your pack."

His laugh was sharp and surprised. "My *pack*?"

"Well, yes. We're making a pack."

"How do you know I want to do that?"

Pica raised her eyebrows at him.

"Fine. Well, if we do, we're not going to live with your family."

"Obviously. That's the point of making a new pack."

"But ... why? Are you sure?"

"Not really," she replied honestly. "This is new for me. I just knew I had to come back to you."

"Well ..." Scruff paused, looking away. Then he looked back at her and said, hesitantly, "Okay."

"It's not completely selfless, you know. I like hanging out with you."

"Me, too."

Pica began to feel uncomfortable, and got back to business. "The main thing to decide is where we're going to live."

"You're moving so quickly!" Scruff laughed, then thought about it. "That's a tough one. There isn't a lot of good territory around here that hasn't already been claimed. Most of what is left is either smaller, unconnected patches of green or the busy parts of the city."

"Way to start out with a positive attitude," Pica laughed. "Are you having doubts already? Scared to be in my pack?"

"Oh, now it's *your* pack, is it?"

Pica smiled. "Well, so far I'm the only one with the good ideas."

"Good ideas?" Scruff snorted. "Your good idea is what? That we wander around randomly trying to find somewhere to live? I definitely have better ideas than that."

"Okay, then. What do you think we should do?"

"I'll only tell you if we call it my pack."

"I'll only decide when I hear your idea."

Scruff shook his head, rolling his eyes, looking happier than she had seen him in a long time. "Fine. Remember when I was telling you about Mala? She was that old coyote who told me how to get back across the highway. Well, she originally came from this place on the other side of the bridge — she called it the Wild Lands. I could barely see it from where I was standing on the beach, but she knew about it because she had been born there. She said that it was different, fewer humans, and that there was lots of territory available."

Pica considered this for a moment. "What do you think that means, *wild*? I mean, how is it different than here?"

"I'm not sure. But I want to find out."

"What about Storm?"

Scruff nodded. "Yes, that's a problem. But I think I know a way to get there that doesn't involve passing through their territory."

Pica frowned, and then realized what he was saying. "No. I'm not swimming. I've never even tried it — I'll drown for sure."

"No, you won't. It's instinctual. Anyway, we can stick close to the shoreline and take breaks. It will just help us stay out of the way."

Pica hesitated a moment, then responded, "Okay."

"Okay?"

"Yup. I'm in."

"All right." Scruff smiled, feeling excited for the first time that he could remember. "So, what about your family, then?"

"Well, I'll obviously tell them about my decision."

"They won't be happy."

"Probably not. But they love me, and anyway, we both know that pups don't always stay with their parents. It's not uncommon for a few to go off and start a new pack."

"With the coyote who killed their father?"

Pica's face became serious. "Don't joke about that. I know you didn't plan to be involved, but I still can't really think about it. I hope once we find somewhere new to live we can move past it."

"Sorry. It's really hard for me, too. I just can't quite believe that this is happening."

"I know. I was going to head back home, but I just ended up here. I think, on some level, I knew that I needed to be with you."

"Well, I feel like that, too."

"All right, it's settled. Tonight we go back, tell my family, and then we can set out."

"I don't think I should go with you."

"You don't have to come right up and kiss them. Feel free to keep your distance. But I think we should travel together from now on. It's safer, and I want to."

"Fine. I can already see who will be calling the shots in our pack."

Pica just smiled and curled up against him, her breath slowly matching his. They lay together for a few moments, each thinking about the sudden new direction their lives were taking. Then they rose and began the journey back to Pica's family. They trotted together as if choreographed, Scruff falling in just behind Pica, their legs moving at almost the same time.

Breaking the news to her family was not easy. Pica left Scruff a short distance away and returned on her own. It took quite a while to round everyone up because they had already started their evening hunt. Finally, everyone was assembled. As Pica spoke, their relief at seeing her again turned into concern and anger.

"How could you make a pack with *him*?" Kai burst out angrily.

"Him?" Pica replied, equally sharply. "You mean the one whose mother died because of us, and who happened to be there when Jagger killed our father? Is that the *him* that you hate so much?"

Kai was silent. Sage spoke next. "I don't want you to leave."

This one was harder. "Sage, I still love all of you. I just feel like I need to move on."

Dane walked over and nuzzled both of them. "I understand. I have been thinking of moving on, too. It doesn't mean that we'll never see each other again. Things change — they have to." He looked Pica straight in the eyes. "If you want to form a pack with Scruff, then I'm okay with it. As long as you're happy."

"I am." Pica felt relieved. Dane had always been on her side, though. She still had yet to make eye contact with her mother.

"Pica." Gree's voice was soft. "I'm not really surprised." Pica lifted her head with surprise, looking at her mother. The loving expression on her face was almost enough to bring Pica to tears. Gree continued, "I've seen how you two play — even as pups, you were so alike. I'm sorry that things happened the way they did, but if you want to join him and start a pack, I accept that. I don't want him around here, but I want you to be happy, and I think that you can be, with him."

Pica breathed a sigh of relief. She hadn't expected this. They all stood awkwardly. Taba finally broke the silence. "Where is he?"

Pica motioned her head. "Waiting for me back there." Gree sighed. "You should probably go then."

Now that it was the time to leave them, Pica had a flash of regret. After all this time, she had finally found them again. Why was she leaving? Before she could lose her resolve, she began her final goodbye howl. It began low and quiet, and got louder as she threw her head back. Soon, she heard her mother's and her siblings' voices join in, weaving around each other in an ancient melody. They sang out their grief, their worry, and their sadness. Slowly, the others trailed off until it was just Pica. Her final note rung out in the cold winter air. Then, everything said in those notes, she walked away from her family.

TWENTY-SIX
A NEW LIGHT

Pica

The ground dropped off underneath her feet, and then, far beneath her, there was only water. She followed the narrow metal path, keeping up a steady trot. Cold air ruffled her fur, and every few moments, a car passed on the other side of the barrier to her left, pushing a wall of air at her. She stopped briefly to look down at the ocean. It was a big dark eye, with the moon highlighting the flecks in its iris. She could smell the salt. It wasn't long until she saw ground underneath the pathway again, and caught its earthy, loamy smell. All she could see ahead of her were trees, standing tall, dark sentinels of the night. She looked behind her and smiled. Scruff smiled back. Then, she began the descent toward her new life.

Scruff

The ground dropped off underneath his feet, and then, far beneath him, there was only water. He followed the narrow metal path, keeping up a steady trot. Cold air ruffled his fur, and every few moments, a car passed on the other side of the barrier to his left, pushing a wall of air at him. He stopped briefly to look down at the ocean. It was a big dark eye, with the moon highlighting the flecks in its iris. He could smell the salt. It wasn't long until he saw ground underneath the pathway again, and caught its earthy, loamy smell. All he could see ahead of him were trees, standing tall, dark sentinels of the night. Pica looked back and smiled at him. He smiled back. Then, he began the descent toward his new life.

ACKNOWLEDGEMENTS

They say it takes a village to raise a child. I found the same is true for writing a book.

Here is my village.

Kristin McHale and Barbara Bradford. Champions of the book from the beginning and the first two people to set eyes on the finished manuscript. Thank you for your sage advice and your endless corrections of comma splices and repeated words.

Don Bailey. My guide and mentor through this process of "writing a book." Thank you for all of your words of wisdom, including telling me to "get started on the sequel already!"

Sathya Siva. The first kid to read my book. Thank you for giving me the best compliment possible: that you couldn't put it down. Nothing could have been more encouraging.

My "Coyote" People: Janet Kessler and her *Coyote Yipps* blog inspire me every day, bringing the lives of urban coyotes alive in stunning detail; Dan Straker and Greg Hart of the Stanley Park Ecology Society coordinate a co-existing with coyotes program that provided me with ample anecdotes for the story; Janelle VanderBeek at the Wildlife Rescue Association of B.C. showed me where they rehabilitate coyotes and allowed me to bring that section of the book to life; and Alessandro Massolo at the University of Calgary gave freely of his time to help me understand what coyote habitats look like, and showed me the cutest video of coyote pups I've ever seen.

The Dundurn team, especially Scott Fraser, who took the leap of faith because Pica and Scruff wouldn't leave him alone. Laura Boyle and the artistic team created an absolutely perfect front cover, and Shannon Whibbs edited with a keen and careful eye.

The many members of my loving family, both in B.C. and Washington. In particular, Hannah, Mom, and Dad, my nuclear nest. Thank you for your constant and unconditional support in the form of (amongst many other things) baby-holding, hugs, coffee runs, funny cards, and late-night texts.

Seth. I couldn't have finished this project (and had so much fun doing it) without such strong support. You wore all the hats: cheerleader, editor, critic, sounding board, coyote spotter, and tech-support master. Thank you for doing this and more with intelligence, generosity, and love.

Finally, Zoe. I finished writing this story while pregnant with you and got my publishing contract as I welcomed you into the world. This book is dedicated to you, birthed together with this project. May your imagination be rich and your heart full.

Book Credits

Acquisitions Editor: Scott Fraser
Project Editor: Jenny McWha
Editor: Shannon Whibbs

Designer: Laura Boyle

Publicist: Elham Ali